Over the Divide

Catherine Farnes

BJU PRESS
Greenville, South Carolina

Library of Congress Cataloging-in-Publication Data

Farnes, Catherine, 1964-
    Over the divide / Catherine Farnes.
        p. cm.
Summary: While leading twelve backpackers on a particularly difficult
wilderness trip in south central Montana, fifteen-year-old Jacy and her
father begin to realize that God is trying to draw them to Himself.
    ISBN 1-57924-646-X (perfect bound paperback : alk. paper)
    [1. Backpacking—Fiction. 2. Camping—Fiction. 3. Interpersonal
relations—Fiction. 4. Conversation—Fiction. 5. Self-reliance—Fiction.
6. Montana—Fiction.] I. Title.

    PZ7.F238265 Ov 2001
    [Fic]—dc21   2001001501

Over the Divide

Cover and Design by TJ Getz

© 2001 Bob Jones University Press
Greenville, SC 29614

ISBN 1-57924-646-X

15   14   13   12   11   10   9   8   7   6   5   4   3   2   1

For Gary Brown and Ernest Farnes,
who have made a love for these mountains
and of God's awesome creation
a part of their children's,
and now their grandchildren's,
heritage.

Books by Catherine Farnes

The Rivers of Judah Series
    Rivers of Judah
    Snow
    Out of Hiding
    The Way of Escape

Over the Divide

Contents

CHAPTER 01

"Whose idea was this, anyway?"

I smiled at the question and at the girl who'd asked it. Sophie Sullivan was her name, and she was exactly the kind of girl that inspired men to hold stubbornly onto the claim that hiking was a guy thing. In the two hours since she and her family had arrived at our place for their scheduled trip, she'd done nothing but complain, swish her hair, and ask me how on earth I, a fellow female, lived for six days out of a backpack. I'd done my best to instruct her, but she was still insisting that she *needed* everything she had brought along. I handed her a rain poncho—something she really would need—and said, "I think I heard your dad say it's been a dream of your family's forever."

"His dream, maybe." She huffed and then yanked her clothes out of her pack. Again. "I'm never going to fit all this in here."

"Leave some of it," I suggested for what had to be the twentieth time.

She scowled at me. "Right, Jacy. That's your name, right? Anyway, maybe if my clothes were as ordinary as yours, I wouldn't care. But they're not."

My younger brother Dakota stepped in behind me and held one of our prepacked plastic pouches out to Sophie. "This has matches, water purification tablets, a roll of toilet paper, and your very own bottle of biodegradable soap in it. You'll want to pack this near the top of your pack, and you'll want to not be wasteful." He bent and looked into her pack. "You can't use the shampoo you brought because it'll damage the environment so you might as well leave it." He grinned as he reached into her pack to pull out a curling iron.

A curling iron!

Did this girl think there was a bed and breakfast at the top of the Continental Divide?

Dakota tossed the curling iron onto Sophie's still-open suitcase. "There's no electricity."

She rolled her eyes. "It has batteries."

Dakota laughed even though Sophie had obviously embarrassed him.

But he needn't have been embarrassed. Who'd ever heard of a curling iron with batteries? And what kind of person went on a wilderness adventure and still worried about her hair? I suspected that by the end of the trip, Sophie's hair would be the least of her concerns. It would definitely be the least of mine. "After six days without a shower," I said, "you're going to be as ordinary as the rest of us no matter what you do to your hair."

"I don't think so," she said.

Dakota and I left Sophie alone with her ego. It was our job to distribute gear to the hikers, and Sophie was only one of them. Her parents and younger sister Candice were also along for the trip, as were two guys from Germany who had obviously done lots of backpacking, and a young couple on their honeymoon who had never been to the mountains.

The two hikers I was most curious about though were Pastor Bruce Adams and his son Ezra. The pastor had met my father on a river rafting trip in Idaho last summer. For reasons that Dad still hadn't completely unveiled to Dakota and me, they had begun a friendship there that seemed to go beyond two guys bonding over a mutual challenge. Dad didn't talk about it much, and Dakota and I didn't press him.

Dad hadn't talked much about anything since Mom's death eight years ago.

But I was curious. Considering how angry Dad was on account of Mom dying, at God or fate or whatever, what could he possibly have in common with a pastor?

I suspected that Dakota and I were both secretly hoping to find out during this hike. I knew I was.

Unfortunately, Sophie and her sister held about as much promise for allowing a peaceful and enlightening hike as if we were going to be leading a group of preschoolers—even though they were teenagers like Dakota and me.

"I can't believe I'm going to sleep on the ground" was Candice's chief lament. That, and "Six days without TV . . ."

Sophie, of course, had concerns of her own. "I hope nobody important e-mails me while I'm gone," and "We're going to smell so gross."

Whine. Whine. Whine.

That's all the two of them did.

Except when they were bragging.

"Did you know that our daddy flies for . . ." *Bla, bla, bla.*

"Our summer house on the lake is bigger than this place . . ." *Bla, bla, bla.*

"You'd think with as much money as we paid to be here, we'd have horses to carry our packs for us."

Bla, bla, bla.

"Then you wouldn't be backpacking," their father pointed out. He seemed like a nice enough guy. I wondered how he'd ended up raising such snobby kids.

Oh well. It was nothing new to have at least one somewhat spoiled person on one of our trips.

My father, Mr. Hayden Craig, advertised himself as an adventure leader. He made his living by taking groups of people on weeklong backpacking treks during the summer, outfitting and guiding hunting groups of big bucks paying trophy-seeking tourists from back east during the fall, and showing out-of-staters all the back trails on snowmobiles during the winter.

Back Trails Unlimited: Guided Hunts and Hikes, he'd called our business. *Adventure Far from the City Lights.*

We had definitely been far from the city lights since the year after Mom's death. That's when we'd moved to our cabin in the mountain town where Dad had grown up. Dad had spent most of the first year stocking up on equipment, securing advertising, and building two bunk rooms onto the house. And then we'd opened for business and hadn't slowed down since. Dad had "guessed" correctly that a lot of people would want to experience the great outdoors if they could do so with an experienced guide. Dad provided all the equipment. He did all the planning. He saw to all the details. All a customer had to do to begin his adventure was make a reservation to be part of one of our fifteen-person parties—including Dad, Dakota, and me—and show up at our door with a sturdy pair of hiking boots.

We scheduled several six-day hikes each summer depending on the weather. We used the off weeks to clean and reorganize the gear for the next trip and for taking people on smaller excursions. Four-wheel-driving or ATV-ing the old mining roads behind town or across the Morrison Jeep Trail. Day hikes to Granite Peak, Liver Eatin' Johnson's old claim, or Grasshopper Glacier.

"How come I have to carry my own plate?" Sophie Sullivan asked my father when he came into the room. "I thought you were supposed to do all that."

Dad shoved his handkerchief down into his back pocket and wasted no time about answering Sophie. "You are paying me to keep you on the trail," he said. "And to take care of a bear should one come into camp. And to stop you if you try to shove a handful of poisonous berries into your mouth. And to make sure you don't miss any of the sights because you're too busy worrying about the dirt under your fingernails." He laughed, but only for an instant before his face went stern again. "You're not paying me to carry your plate."

4

Even though it wasn't the friendliest version of Let's-get-this-understood-before-we-leave-in-the-morning-because-we're-not-going-to-have-time-for-it-after-that, it was effective.

Sophie muttered something that sounded like *sorry* and Dad continued about his business.

He made sure everyone had brought enough pairs of dry socks.

He checked to see that nobody had packed his or her rain poncho at the bottom of the pack.

He assigned Pastor Adams and the other adult hikers a can of concentrated pepper spray and then went around the room inspecting everyone's hiking boots. "It's been a wet year," he said. "There are places on the trail that are going to be muddy, if not under water. If your boots get wet and don't fit you just right, they'll rub and you'll get some nasty blisters." He paid particular attention to Sophie's and Candice's boots since they had already distinguished themselves as Trail Whiners. If there was one thing that tested Dad's ordinarily controlled and detached professionalism, it was whining.

"I'm sure Daddy got nothing but the best for his little princesses," Dakota whispered to me.

I elbowed him. Hard. Snobs or not, Sophie and Candice were our customers. It was a good thing for us that there were people who could afford to hire Dad to guide them and did hire him even though the trail could be hiked without cost by any Joe or Jane with a backpack.

The trail was thirty-two miles through some of the most beautiful and pristine country on earth. It cut across part of the Absaroka-Beartooth Wilderness from Cooke Pass to East Rosebud in south central Montana, right near the northeast entrance of Yellowstone National Park. All at about ten thousand feet.

"Are you thinking on covering about five miles a day?" Pastor Adams asked Dad.

"Pretty much."

"Is the trail thirty-two miles as the crow flies or including all the switchbacks?" the young husband asked.

Dad only grinned.

"The actual distance is not important, yes," said one of the men from Germany. "Because it will feel like fifty miles either way you look at it."

"Great," Sophie muttered.

She had gotten Dad's attention again. "It'll feel like a hundred if you have a bad attitude," he said. "And not only that, you'll make it feel like a thousand for the rest of us."

The annoyance to my father of a snobby teenager's dislike for him would be nothing compared to the annoyance for Sophie should Dad decide to return the sentiment. I was about to tell her quietly that she'd be wise to stay on his good side when there was a tap at our front door.

"That'll be D'Ary," Dad said to Dakota and me. He looked over at Sophie and her sister, and I knew exactly what he was thinking. This was a scheduling oversight—an outright blunder— if ever he'd been guilty of one.

Dakota missed Dad's concern entirely. He grinned and said, "Leave him waiting a minute. I love making these people who never have to wait for anything wait for me."

My father was a rugged individualist. He always had been. A little abrasive on the outside but decent when it counted and un- questionably competent. He had to be gruff, he'd told me more than once, so that there wouldn't be any debate about who was in charge in a critical split second if anything unexpected happened.

And he was good at being gruff. But he wasn't a jerk.

"Open the door, Dakota," he said.

Dakota did.

The young man who stepped tentatively inside held his hand out first to Dakota and then to Dad.

"Good trip over?" Dad asked him.

"Yes, sir. Thank you."

I watched as Sophie nearly stumbled backward over a boxed-up cookstove in order to whisper something to Candice. I watched our young husband glance in recognition at the newest addition to our hiking party.

Neil D'Ary.

Sophie's parents obviously had no idea who Neil was and neither did the guys from Germany. I couldn't tell for sure about the young wife or Pastor Adams and Ezra.

"This is Neil," Dad said. "He's going to be hiking the trail with us this week."

"I knew it!" Sophie squealed. "I knew it! You're Neil D'Ary the tennis player! I saw you when I was watching Wimbledon, and—"

"Wimbledon," Neil muttered.

"Yeah." Sophie's right hand went to her mouth. "That's what I said. I'm, like, your biggest fan. I think you're so awesome."

She kept blabbering after that, but all I could do was pity Neil D'Ary.

Dad and Dakota and I had hosted famous people before. Not often, but often enough to know that most of them came on trips like this in places like this to get away from people like Sophie.

"As far as I've ever been able to tell," Dad liked to say, "we all need a bathroom and we all have bad breath in the morning. We're pretty much the same when it comes right down to it."

Crude, but accurate.

I'd seen the truth of it in many of the people who had come to adventure with us. Most of them had money. Lots of it. Yet none of them seemed free of problems because of it. Besides that, four to seven days in the mountains had a way of bringing even the most arrogant of people around to the reality of their insignificance in the greater scheme of things.

The rocks on the slope of a mountain couldn't care less if it was Jane Doe walking over them or the President of the United States . . . though Dad had told me recently that he'd read where they'd cry out praise to Jesus if people refused to worship Him.

An avalanche would just as quickly flatten the World's Strongest Man if he got in its path as it would anyone else. Or nobody at all. The snow would be oblivious either way.

If the sky wanted to hail, it would do it whether or not the Academy Award Winning Actress or the Most Beloved News Anchor had made it to the other side of the clearing.

If there was a God—which I was still undecided about—I suspected that He wouldn't be impressed by the things that impressed most people.

Neil D'Ary, for instance. He could hit a little bright ball with a racket and make it go anywhere he wanted it to go as quickly or slowly as he wanted it to go there, and he'd made a lot of money during the last year doing that even though he was barely eighteen years old. Impressive? Definitely. Phenomenal, even.

But if there was a God, He had made the sun, the grizzly bear, the human eye. What was being able to hit a little bright ball in comparison to that?

And Sophie Sullivan. She had strolled into our place as if she were the queen of the Nile and we should all bow down in grateful homage or at the very least carry her silverware! But now she was the one doing obeisance, making an idiot of herself idolizing someone she didn't even know except that she'd seen him on TV hitting his little bright ball with a racket.

This was going to be an interesting six days. No question about it.

I walked across the room and introduced myself to Neil D'Ary. "Come on," I said when I'd let go of his hand, "I'll get you set up with a pack."

Mr. Sullivan had his hands full trying to pilot his girls' dinner conversation beyond the topic of Neil D'Ary. Since our meals for the next few days would be coming out of vacuum sealed plastic bags, I had taken Pastor and Ezra Adams, our honeymooners, and the Sullivan family into Cooke City for one final fat and calorie and cheese-filled meal. With pop. And dessert. The two men from Germany had preferred to stay at the cabin. So had Neil D'Ary.

"He's just another person," Mr. Sullivan said after Sophie had made a remark—her fourth or fifth—about not being able to wait to tell her friends at the country club that she had hiked thirty-whatever miles with Neil D'Ary. "A person, I might add, who doesn't seem to appreciate your ridiculous attention."

"I'm sure he's used to it. I mean, he's only the most gorgeous guy to walk onto a tennis court in—"

Pastor Adams set his glass down. "Famous or not, Neil D'Ary is a human being just like the rest of us. He may be as needy on the inside as the next guy."

"Is that all you religious people ever think about?" Since Pastor Adams wasn't the only one to look at her in semidisgust, Sophie added, "I mean, you know, it's not like you'd just go ask him 'Are you needy on the inside?' even if he was a nobody."

"Nobody is a nobody," Ezra said.

"Whatever."

"I read somewhere that Neil's dad is really controlling," Candice said. "I heard one of the announcers talking about how his mom can't stand to go to tournaments and watch him because—"

"That's the action-packed nature of tennis for you if the announcers have time to talk about stuff like that," I said.

Sophie leaned in toward the table. "I read that he's allergic to bee stings and that he likes pork chops and that his favorite color is green."

"You know what I read?" I waited for both girls to look at me. "I read that a telepathic hamster moved Scrabble squares around and predicted that Neil would be famous even before he was born."

"You did not read that!" Sophie said. She was laughing.

"I think," said Mr. Sullivan, "that what Jacy is trying to say is that you can't believe everything you read in the media, and that you shouldn't feel like you know this kid just because you've read things."

Candice nodded tolerantly. Then she said, "I bet Neil has to have epinephrine with him all the time."

"Are there bees up here?"

"That would be really scary."

"If anything happens," Sophie said, "I know how to do mouth-to-mouth resuscitation."

Pastor Adams set his glass down again. Firmly. He didn't say anything, but I certainly wouldn't have minded if he had.

Something along the lines of *That comment was completely inappropriate* or *For all you know, this kid could be a real creep and you guys are acting like he's some kind of god.* There was probably even some Bible verse he could have quoted.

Apparently, though, the pastor was content to let Candice and Sophie's consciences do the talking. Either that or he was hoping their father would.

I didn't have that much confidence in their consciences, so when Mr. Sullivan only sighed and shook his head, I said, "I can't believe you guys. I hope you'll have the decency to leave him alone so he can enjoy his trip. You know, don't ask him to sign your bottle of sunscreen." Then just so they'd know, I added, "Neil is allergic to bee stings." I looked steadily at Sophie. "But my dad'll be taking charge of any medical emergencies, thanks."

"We'll pray that there won't be any." Pastor Adams stared at me for several moments before picking up his roll to butter it. "I'm sure your father knows how to handle them though."

I nodded. Should I tell them about the guy who'd stumbled and broken his leg twelve miles from anywhere? Or about the lady who had decided to "bathe" in Fossil Lake before anyone else was awake and had barely been able to drag herself out of the water before going numb from hypothermia? Should I mention all the minor cuts, bruises, cases of altitude sickness, and twisted ankles that my father had known exactly how to handle? No. Details would probably only frighten them. True, a small amount of healthy fear could work to one's benefit in the mountains. True, it might be amusing to watch their faces pale when I mentioned the woman who had taken food into her tent and had lost a sizable chunk of her right upper arm to a griz who'd sniffed it out. But I decided that it would suffice to assure them that my father would know exactly what to do for Neil D'Ary if he did get stung by a bee and for anyone else who might get hurt in any way during the hike.

After dinner I escorted the two girls and their parents through all the town's gift and souvenir shops and the General Store. Pastor Adams, Ezra, and the honeymooners had chosen instead to walk up toward the dump because Pastor Adams had read somewhere that black bears frequented the place. I didn't tell them whether bears did or did not visit our dump or that they'd have to wait for dark to have any real shot at sighting a bear. This was their adventure. If they wanted to waste it looking around a dump, that was their business. It wasn't as if perusing gift shops would have been any more exciting for them. It certainly wasn't exciting for me, listening to Sophie and Candice prattle on about how Tatiana would just love this and wouldn't Gabrielle just die over

that and what did you say Neil's favorite color is? . . . green? . . .
I might have to pick up a new shirt.

I chatted with the shop owners or the college kids they'd hired
to help man the counters during the busy summer tourist season.
I bought a few hard candy sticks. I waved hello to Gary when he
drove by us in the wrecker hauling another minivan. Someone
had undoubtedly tried to take it up one of the old mining roads.
Not an informed decision. I even attempted a real conversation
with Sophie and Candice while we waited outside the café for
Pastor Adams and the newlyweds.

No go, though.

I was just the hired guide.

Not even the hired guide. The hired guide's daughter.

Oh well. There was nothing I'd rather be—no other life I'd
rather have. I loved the mountains. I loved working with Dad.
And I loved meeting people from all over the world and helping
them experience my little piece of it.

Living in such a small town and mainly a tourist town did
have its disadvantages though. Very few people stayed around all
year because the winters were so brutal. Of those who did live
here permanently, nobody was my age. Things were more difficult to get. More expensive, usually. Everything in town was
geared toward visitors, so if we needed anything practical, like
new socks, and we didn't want to pay three times the price for the
ones with elk embroidered on the sides, we'd have to make a trip
either through the park to Gardiner or down the Beartooth
Highway or over Dead Indian Hill to Billings. A day's endeavor
one way or the other.

But any way we drove it, the trip was gorgeous. Since I hadn't
always lived in these mountains, I didn't take it for granted. The
view I saw out my bedroom window each morning that I was
home to see it was a view that many people would only see once
in their lives and that most people would never see at all. Life was
clean and uncomplicated. I never worried about whether or not

my shoes were the right brand or color, only whether or not they were functional.

And I was almost never bored. How could I be? Our work was work, but it was exciting. Challenging. Never the same two days in a row.

I stood up and grinned when I saw Pastor Adams, Ezra, and the newlyweds coming toward us. "Did you see anything?" I asked them.

"Garbage," the wife said.

"It is a dump," I reminded her. *What a way to spend your honeymoon, honey. How romantic!* "They've pretty much started making the bins bearproof. It's not good for bears to get used to associating us with food."

Pastor Adams smiled. "I guess it wouldn't be."

CHAPTER 03

Dad and I were sitting on the front deck railing later that evening when we saw headlights coming up our driveway through the trees.

"We don't have anyone else for this trip, do we?" I asked.

"No." He slid from the railing and stood at the top of the steps with his hands shoved into his jacket pockets. He muttered, "Fancy," when the car pulled slowly into the clearing at the bottom of our 'lawn' and the headlights went dark. "Seen it before?"

"No," I said.

"Didn't think so." He pulled his handkerchief out of his back pocket, coughed into it, and shoved it into his pocket again. "I haven't either."

We waited and watched while the driver stepped out of his shiny black car and walked up the dirt path toward the steps.

"Evening," Dad called to him.

The man was big. Intimidating. Dressed all in black except for the thick gold chain hanging from his neck and the jewel-laden watch on his wrist. The sun had already gone behind the trees so I couldn't see perfectly, but the man's posture and pace made it plain that his reason for dropping by wasn't casual. He didn't return Dad's greeting.

Dad started down the stairs. "Is there something I can do for you?"

"Yeah," he answered when he'd gotten even with Dad on the stairs. "I'm Quentin D'Ary. I'm looking for my son."

When the man tried to push his way past him, Dad stepped in front of him again. "I don't know about where you're from, sir, but around here people generally wait to be invited before walking into a guy's house."

"This is some kind of outfitting place, isn't it?" Mr. D'Ary waved his hand in front of his face as he made several mocking attempts at our slogan. Finally he got it right. "Adventure far from the city lights."

"Yeah, that's us," Dad said. "But this is also my home." He gave Mr. D'Ary a couple seconds to think about that. "Is Neil expecting you?"

"I don't see how that's any of your business."

Dad shrugged. "Just asking."

"Well, don't," Mr. D'Ary said. "Just go tell him I'm here."

After a moment Dad nodded at me and I went inside to find Neil. Because of a comment Neil had made to me while I was showing him how to adjust the shoulder straps on his pack, I suspected that he would not be glad of the news that he had company, especially this particular company. I made sure none of the other hikers were listening when I told him and then followed him back out to the front deck.

Sure enough, Neil's reaction to seeing his father was about as warm as nightfall in February. His shoulders stiffened. His face showed frustration. His voice was strained even though he only said, "Sir."

"I don't figure I can talk you out of this?" Mr. D'Ary asked, but it sounded more like a whiny statement.

"No, sir."

"Then I'm coming with you." Mr. D'Ary glared at Neil for several moments, his eyes forbidding any argument.

"Fine," Neil finally said. "Sir."

Mr. D'Ary turned to Dad. "You've got room for one more, haven't you, Outback Jack?"

"I guess I do," Dad said. "Just. And the name's Hayden Craig."

"My things are in the trunk." Mr. D'Ary pulled a set of keys out of his pocket and held it out to Dad. "Hayd."

Dad turned away from the big man's outstretched hand. "Better get after them if we're going to get your pack set up at a reasonable hour." Then he went inside the house.

When Mr. D'Ary started moving his keys in my direction, I laughed and shook my head. "Now's as good a time as any to start carrying your own stuff. You'll be doing it all week."

Neil looked away from me when I walked past him and inside.

I found my father in the supply room. He was sorting through the packs, trying to find one large enough to accommodate Mr. D'Ary. "You could have told him we didn't have room," I said.

"Why would I do that, Jace?" He stopped what he was doing to stand and look right at me. "This is a business. If he can pay his way, which he obviously can, I've got no good reason to turn him away." He held up his hand before I could even get my mouth open. "Whatever's between them is none of our business."

Dad usually wasn't one to defend his decisions like that, so I suspected that he wasn't any more comfortable about having Mr. D'Ary along than I was.

But he was right. This was a business. And Dad was an adventure guide not a social worker.

Besides, six days in the mountains together could prove to be good for Neil D'Ary and his dad . . . if someone could figure out how to keep Sophie and Candice out of their way.

Maybe I'd talk to their father.

Maybe I'd talk directly to them.

I chose a sleeping bag and one of our thicker roll-up mats for Mr. D'Ary and scolded myself. I wouldn't talk to anyone. My father was right about one other thing: whatever was between Neil and his father was none of my business. I'd probably only mess things up if I meddled.

But that didn't mean I couldn't hope that the trail would take care of Sophie and Candice. It would be difficult for them to keep rambling on about tennis if they could barely breathe on account of the combination of uphill and ever thinning air.

Even if the girls packed up and went home tonight, it wouldn't guarantee anything anyway. Neil and his father might spend the whole six days avoiding one another or fighting with one another or talking meaninglessly about porcupines and whether or not fish survived during the winter in frozen-over lakes.

"None of my business," I whispered to myself. Louder and to Dad I said, "Should I give Mr. D'Ary his own tent?"

"Might be an idea."

"How do you suppose things got so sour between them?"

Dad answered right away. "None of my business."

"Right."

He smiled and tossed a rain poncho to me. "Or yours."

"I know." I caught the rain poncho and balanced it on top of Mr. D'Ary's growing stack of gear. "It bugs me, is all." I shrugged. Since it was bound to sound syrupy no matter how I said it, I said it in a syrupy sing-song voice. It was just more comfortable that way. "I can't imagine not being close to my dad."

Dad tapped me on the head with an empty plastic water bottle. "How sweet." He held onto the water bottle when I tried to grab it from him, and we laughed and tugged back and forth at it for a couple of minutes.

"Well," Dad said when he finally surrendered the water bottle and stood to start filling the pack he'd chosen with all the gear I'd chosen, "let's hope D'Ary really came prepared to hike." He shouldered the pack and walked out toward the front room. "He'd be quite the sight up there in those shiny black shoes he's got on."

"He'd be an accident waiting to happen." I locked the door before pulling it shut behind me.

While Dad and Dakota helped Mr. D'Ary get his pack ready and told him all the rules of the trail—pack it in pack it out, no cans or plastic in the campfire, no food in the tents, no illegal drugs, Dad's in charge—I went back out to the front deck to see if Neil was still there.

He was. Sitting on the bottom step tossing pebbles onto the dirt path.

"Mind if I join you?" I asked him.

"It's your house," he said after looking over his shoulder to see who I was.

"Get simple for me, Neil," I said. "Yes or no. Do you mind if I join you?"

He smiled, but only for a second before turning away. "No. I don't mind."

I sat on the same step as he but not close to him. I wanted to make sure he understood that I wasn't just another idiot looking to be as near as possible to "the most gorgeous guy to step onto a tennis court in decades" or whatever Sophie had said. "In a couple of hours," I told him, "the sky will be full of stars. Sometimes I go lie in the grass and just stare up at them. After a while you realize that there's no place that's black. Behind the bright stars are dimmer ones and there are dimmer ones still behind those and they just go on that way forever."

"It must be something, living up here," he said after a while.

I didn't comment. Not everyone would like it.

"Do you ever have bears around?" he asked.

"Yeah. If we don't clean the grill real good, they'll come up on the back deck."

"Really?"

I nodded.

He smiled and shook his head. "I think I'd be keeping my grill inside."

"That's even worse," I told him. "Then they try to get in after it."

"Okay," he said. "So I wouldn't have a grill."

"You could have a grill. You just need a gun too. A really big one."

"Could you shoot a bear?" he asked me. "For real?"

I had to think about that. "I suppose I would if it was attacking Dakota or Dad or something. I think I'd try to scare it away first. I mean, they have as much right to live in these mountains as we do."

"Just not in your house," Neil said.

"Exactly."

"Have you ever seen a bear on the trail we'll be hiking?"

I nodded.

"Close up or far away?"

I shuddered. "Way too close up. It was attacking one of our hikers in the middle of the night."

"Wow. What happened?"

"Dad shot it." I shrugged. "It was a dangerous bear. The same one had mauled someone in the park only a few weeks before. It would have been killed eventually anyway. They kill people-killing bears."

"Sounds like you don't like that very much."

"That was perceptive." I smiled. "I know Dad didn't like doing it, but he didn't have a choice really. I mean, she could have killed that lady and more of us if he hadn't done it. Still, they're just animals doing what animals do. That lady shouldn't have brought food inside her tent."

Neil looked down at the dirt. "Just a person doing what people do. Botching it."

Sensing that that comment was about much more than a lady bringing food into her tent in the middle of bear country, but feeling inadequate to pursue it beyond that, I leaned back on the steps and stared up at the sky.

"Do you like tennis?" Neil asked me.

I decided I might as well be honest. "Not really." I kept looking at the sky. "Do you?"

He laughed. "Now *that* was perceptive."

He would have said more I was certain, but the door opened behind us and our fathers joined us on the steps.

After that Neil didn't say a word.

CHAPTER **04**

"These mosquitoes are completely out of control," Candice complained for what had to be the fortieth time in fewer than ten minutes.

"That's because it's been a wet year," I told her. I didn't have the heart to tell her that it was going to get worse once we got out onto the marshes beyond the first lake. "Just swing your baseball cap back and forth in front of you."

"It's bad enough I have to wear this ugly thing."

I bit my tongue and walked past her on the trail to get in line right behind Dad and Pastor Adams. Dad liked for Dakota and me to place ourselves in positions between every four or five hikers. We were supposed to make conversation, keep alert to everyone, and prevent anyone from lagging too far behind. Well, we'd been on the trail for less than an hour so far, hiking over fairly flat ground in the cool of thick forest toward Kersey Lake, so nobody had fallen behind yet. The people that were having problems were being so vocal about them that nobody could miss it. I'd been half tempted to warn them that bears were attracted by the noise of wounded animals in distress. And as for making conversation . . . the two men from Germany were having one of their own—in German. The newlyweds were discussing, debating, tossing around the idea of her having her own checking account, which was definitely none of my business. The Sullivan girls were too busy noticing the weight on their shoulders and hips to engage in conversation. Their parents were too busy telling them to be tough. And Mr. D'Ary and Neil had so engrossed themselves in snubbing one another that neither of them seemed to notice when anyone else was around.

Dakota had already moved to the head of the pack with Dad, Ezra, and the pastor, so I didn't figure it would hurt anything if I did the same.

"The problem I have with what you're saying," Dad was saying to Pastor Adams, "is that it would mean that all the millions of people in the world who aren't Christians are wrong. How can you really know that they're not just as right as you are?"

I heard what Dad was saying underneath his question, and I suspected that Pastor Adams did too. He knew that Dad was a widower.

My wife wasn't a Christian, Adams. If I accept what you're saying, then my only option is to envision her in hell because that's what happens to people when they're wrong in your worldview. I'm not prepared to do that. Not now. Not tomorrow. Not ever.

"I know that there is this main difference between Christianity and every other religion on the planet," Pastor Adams said. "In every other religion, we are trying to earn our way to closeness to God. In Christianity, God . . ."

I stepped in right beside Dakota. "He sure didn't waste any time, did he?"

"It was Dad who brought it up," Dakota whispered back. "Figure that out."

I shrugged in disbelief. "I guess he asked for it then."

And it was clear that Pastor Bruce Adams was not about to pass up such an opportunity. "See, we as people have this problem. We sin. We make mistakes. We do wrong things even when we know they're wrong." He paused a moment. "Do you grant me that?"

I thought of what Neil D'Ary had said about the woman who'd brought food into her tent. *She was just a person doing what people do. Botching it.*

Dad nodded. "Obviously."

"God doesn't do that. He's sinless. Perfect." Another pause. "Do you grant me that?"

"No," Dad said right away. He sounded angry. "I don't grant you that. I don't even grant you that there is a god."

Pastor Adams laughed quietly. "That's all right. You don't need to grant me that yet. If there was a God, do you suppose He'd be perfect?"

"I'd suppose," Dad said, "that he could be however he wanted to be because none of us would be big enough to stop him."

"Fair enough," the pastor said. "But if He was perfect, and if He desired a relationship with us, do you suppose He'd—"

"I don't like supposing, Adams," Dad said. "I like knowing."

"Okay. Then all I can do is tell you what the Bible says, and it's up to you to take it or leave it, which, by the way, is the bottom line of why Christianity is either right or wrong and can't be just one of many different paths to God."

"I know what the Bible says." Dad quickened his pace a little. "I've spent all year reading it."

I leaned toward Dakota and whispered, "I didn't know we even had a Bible."

"Pastor Adams gave one to Dad after that rafting trip," he said. "He showed it to me once."

I had no trouble believing that Pastor Adams would give my father a Bible.

But Dad actually reading it?

That would explain some of the unusual comments he'd been making lately like the one about rocks crying out praise to Jesus.

Pastor Adams kept right up with Dad. "All right. *You* tell *me* what it says."

"From beginning to end," Dad wanted to know, "or just the stuff about Jesus?"

Pastor Adams laughed. "Beginning to end it is about Jesus if you really stop and think about it."

"Okay." Dad took a few moments, maybe an eighth of a mile, to think through what he'd say. "Basically, it's about God, us, and God's continuous attempts to keep us right with Him. First there was the one rule, don't eat the fruit, and we blew it. Then He gave the ten rules, and we were breaking them before Moses even got off the mountain with them. Then there were those two or three books worth of rules which nobody could keep—you know, don't touch dead bodies on the Sabbath and all that. So then there were the sacrifices we could offer to atone for it when we didn't keep them. There were miracles and prophecies and warnings and promises of blessing or punishment." He shrugged. "And then there was Jesus. The ultimate sacrifice. The heavy artillery."

The heavy artillery? What on earth was Dad talking about?

"I was with you till that last statement, Hayden," Pastor Adams said. "Care to explain it?"

"It's almost like God's in a war to get us," Dad said. "He spent the whole Old Testament bending over backwards to help us to keep our covenant with Him. Letting one guy kill hundreds with an animal bone. Making a donkey talk. Stopping the sun in the sky. Torching all those false prophets. Preparing the great fish to swallow Jonah. None of it worked. Not for longer than a generation anyway. So then He sends Jesus. The big gun. Like He's saying, 'You know what? I've done everything I could think of to let you near Me, and you keep wandering off. Now I've sent My Son to make the one-and-only-final-this-is-your-last-chance way for you to be near Me. If you wander away from that, what more can I do?' " Dad grabbed his shoulder straps and repositioned his pack.

"I don't think that would fly from the pulpit," Ezra said.

"I'm not planning on standing behind one."

"You're missing one thing," Pastor Adams said to Dad. "Motivation. Why would God care whether He got us or not? He could always make more. In fact, why didn't He just make us like

24

robots who had no choice but to obey Him? He could have done that."

"Maybe He should have," Dad said.

"That's not love. God wants us to love Him. Your toaster toasting your bread for you isn't doing it because it loves you. It's doing it because that's what it was made to do and it has no choice. That's all it can do." Pastor Adams gave Dad a moment to think about that. "But your children . . . now they can love you. They don't have to. It's not a guarantee. It's a choice they make, and it means all that much more because of that."

"All right," Dad said. "I'll give you that."

"And it's not like God's asking us to give Him anything that He wasn't willing to give for us. I mean, He gave His Son to make the way for us."

"He could have just decided not to have right and wrong," Dad said. "Not to punish wrong."

"Yeah," Pastor Adams said slowly. "Like, say, you deciding not to correct Dakota when he's two and about to stick his finger in a light socket?"

Dad didn't reply.

"Listen, Hayden," Pastor Adams said, "it sounds like you've got more of the information of what the Bible is about than most people do when they pray to receive Christ. But faith is more than an intellectual thing. Getting you to that point of faith is God's job, and I'm more than confident that He can do that." He stayed quiet a while. "I think you read that Bible I gave you because you knew I'd be here this summer asking you about it, and you're not the kind of man who likes to get into a conversation when you don't know what you're talking about. But I can promise you that if you are really interested in seeking out the truth about God, beyond winning a conversation with me, He will reveal Himself to you."

Again Dad stayed quiet.

I wasn't sure, but I thought that I'd be out a few dollars if I had put money on Dad "winning" that conversation. Pastor Adams clearly knew his stuff. And a lot of what he said made sense. Especially the part about faith being more than an intellectual thing and God being the one who had to bring someone to that point of faith.

As we walked, I wondered what sorts of things God—if He was real—would do to bring someone to a point of faith in Him. Would He appear out of our campfire? Would He strike the lake with lightning if I said, "God, if you're real, strike that lake with lightning!"? Would He speak to me in a dream? Would He slowly tear away at everything I *had* put my faith in until He was the only thing left? Would He just softly remind me as I stood at the top of the Continental Divide and looked at all the beauty on every side of me that someone had to have made this?

I did wonder how He would do it, but I didn't know. And I wasn't about to ask Pastor Adams. If my father couldn't hold his own in a conversation with him, I didn't stand a chance!

"We better hold up a little," Dakota said to me. "I can't hear them behind us anymore."

I listened for a moment and then nodded. Dad usually didn't lead out so vigorously. He'd gotten preoccupied with his conversation is all. We hiked the trail six to eight times a summer and were used to the terrain and to the weight on our backs. Except for the two men from Germany, though, and Pastor Adams and Ezra, none of the adventurers on this trip had ever backpacked before. I wasn't concerned about Neil. He was an athlete. He could probably run circles around Dakota and me up these mountains. Maybe around Dad too, though I wouldn't bet on it. But Mr. D'Ary and the newlyweds and the Sullivans would need a slower pace. Especially later when we began the uphill stretch to Russell Lake.

"Dad," I called ahead. "Slow up."

He raised his right hand to let me know he'd heard me just as he, Ezra, and the pastor turned a corner on the trail and went out of view in the thick trees.

The two men from Germany were the first to meet up with Dakota and me. We waved them by, telling them we were going to wait for the others. Neil D'Ary approached us next. He was followed immediately by his father, who was grumbling to himself about what a stupid idea this was because Neil could ruin everything if he injured himself up here . . . and for what?

"That guy really needs to relax," Dakota said when Neil and Mr. D'Ary had gotten far enough past us that they wouldn't hear him.

"He does have a point," I said. "I guess."

"So Neil should never do anything but play tennis because he might get hurt?" Dakota shook his head. "That would stink."

"Hey," I joked, "that's the price you pay if you want to keep making the big bucks. You can't feel too sorry for a guy who can make four hundred thousand dollars in two weeks just for playing a few matches of tennis."

"I'd feel sorry for anyone who had to hike with that guy breathing down his neck like that."

I nodded. Neil D'Ary had not planned to hike this trail with his father. He had initially wanted to schedule earlier in the summer, but Dad required parental consent for kids under eighteen. So Neil had decided to wait until after his birthday in mid-July.

"He won't give me permission," Neil had told my father during their telephone conversation. "He thinks I need to rest up my wrist watching old matches of guys I'll be playing eventually. I've already done that. I've got to get out and do something or I'm going to go nuts."

Dad had given Neil the standard and mandatory you-do-want-to-take-your-father's-advice-into-consideration spiel, but had put Neil down for the first hike in August.

Without a second thought.

Neil would be eighteen then. An adult. Able to make—and be responsible for—his own decisions.

The what's-between-them-is-none-of-my-business thing again.

But I was beginning to taste an uneasy certainty that whatever was between Neil and his father could not remain a secret—or quiet—for six whole days. The tension coming from them was as hard-featured as a moose and was probably as unpredictable.

Anything unpredictable held the potential to result in conflict or carelessness on the trail, or both, which could all too quickly become Dad's business.

"You know what?" I said to Dakota. "You wait for the Sullivans and the newlyweds. I think I'll go walk with the D'Arys."

"Good idea," he said. "Walk *between* them."

CHAPTER 05

Setting up camp that afternoon in the meadows just beyond Russell Lake turned out to be almost as much of a challenge as getting there had been. A thunderstorm had been hanging over-head for a couple of hours but had decided it had had enough of its enormous weight just as we rolled our tents out and began put-ting them up.

It wouldn't have been a problem except that eight of our twelve hikers had never set up a dome tent. Unfamiliarity and clumsiness with the snap-together poles combined with the wind, rain, and noise from the storm to thoroughly unravel the Sullivan girls and provided Mr. D'Ary with one further thing to berate his son about. Dad helped the Sullivans put up their two tents, Dakota helped the newlyweds, I helped Neil, and Pastor Adams and Ezra were gracious enough to assist Mr. D'Ary even though they were under no obligation to do so and could have ducked into their own tent to start getting dry.

"Nothing to do but wait it out," Dad shouted to everyone over the wind. He crawled into our tent and zipped it shut. Then he sat there at the door with his elbows on his knees and his face in his hands.

"You okay, Dad?" Dakota asked him.

"Just tired," he said.

Dakota and I looked at each other across the empty spot on the tent floor where Dad had yet to roll out his sleeping bag. We'd only hiked five miles. The likelihood of Dad being "just tired" was minimal. It was much more probable that all his talking with Pastor Adams about God had started him thinking about Mom which distressed him even now and usually resulted in a brutal headache.

Dakota said, "Lie down for a while, Dad. Jacy and I will get a fire going and see to dinner when the rain lets up."

Dad yanked his sleeping bag out of its sack and spread it out on the floor. He lay down on his stomach without taking off his wet shirt or his boots and said, "Wake me up as soon as it's clear. I want to try to catch some fish. I'm not up to hearing about how nasty the backpacking food is."

I pressed gently at Dad's shoulders near the back of his neck. When he fell asleep after a while, I said, "This isn't what he needs up here, Dakota."

"Maybe one of us should talk to Pastor Adams."

Whenever my brother said *One of us should do such-and-such*, what he really meant was *Jacy, do this*. "All right," I said. "I'll talk to him first chance I get."

It rained for nearly two hours before Dakota and I could slip quietly out of our tent to start preparing dinner for everyone. Since all the wood around had been thoroughly soaked, Dakota dug our two one-burner camp stoves out of Dad's pack, hooked fuel bottles to them, and started boiling some water for the rice pilaf.

"I'm going fishing," I told him. And then I invited Pastor Adams to join me. The sooner he understood that Dad did much better when he didn't talk, think, wonder, dream, or worry about Mom, the better. Especially up here. Especially with the Sullivan girls and the D'Arys behaving the way they were.

"My father spends his whole life looking out for other people," I told the pastor before we'd even gotten down to the lake. "Me and Dakota look out for him."

Pastor Adams listened intently to me and nodded several times as if he understood. But when I finished talking, he said,

"He's only really going to be okay when he deals with the questions inside him."

I stared at the man, barely managing to keep my expression free of the animosity I was beginning to feel. For whatever reason, my father respected this man. And he was a paying customer. I owed it to Dad to treat him civilly. But that didn't mean I couldn't speak my mind. "You don't have the answers to his questions, Pastor Adams," I said coldly. "You only think you do. And you stirring them up is—"

"I don't think I have the answers at all, Jacy," he said. "It's not even about answers. It's about the questions themselves. Acknowledging that you have them. Acknowledging that the fact that you have them and can't readily answer them means that you have need."

He held my fishing pole while I jumped from a ridge onto a boulder at the edge of the water.

"Dealing with that need," he said when he handed me his pole and jumped down, "that's the bottom line. That's what it's about." He sat beside me on the boulder and began to work at untangling his line. "I don't know why your mother got sick or died when she did, but I do know how you can have peace about it. I don't know any of the answers to all the questions your father beats himself up with. You know the ones. The ones that start with *If?*"

Yes. I knew the ones.

But how could a person deal with questions that had no answers apart from tucking them away in some back corner of the mind and ignoring them when they tried to surface? And how could a person truly fill a need that was made up of unanswerable questions?

"I don't understand, Pastor Adams."

"There's only one way that life makes sense," he said, "and that's in the context of belief in God."

"So you're saying that Mom wouldn't have died if we had believed in God?" I shook my head. That was stupid. People who believed in God died all the time.

He smiled. "No. I'm saying that if there were no God, and human beings had somehow managed to beat all the odds and come through all the unlikely progressions of so-called evolution into existence, all our lives would be anyway is being born, living, dying, and ceasing to exist. All of it random. All of it meaningless when it comes right down to it."

"I can see that." Actually, what I saw in my mind was a flash from a vacuum cleaner commercial I'd seen. It featured what was supposed to be magnified-to-the-millionth-degree dust mites swarming through what was supposed to be magnified-to-the-millionth-degree carpet fibers. Completely disgusting. And, as Pastor Adams had said, completely meaningless. Be born to eat to keep yourself alive and maybe move on to bigger, better, and more tasty stretches of flooring before getting old, dying, and rotting away somewhere.

What a bleak outlook.

Haunting, even.

"But how does believing in God make it any different?" I asked the pastor. "Except in maybe making yourself feel better about it."

"It's more than making ourselves feel better," he said. "If there is God, then we're here for a reason. We were created by someone with the capacity to love and create and renew. We are more than the result of some big bang and lightning hitting some pool of primordial soup at just the right instant. If there is God, we can have more than just living and dying. We can have living with a purpose and as part of the greater bigger picture. We can be part of what He's doing." Something tugged at his line and he began to slowly reel in. "If there is God," he said, "we can have peace."

As much as my father had succeeded in pulling himself and our life and business together after Mom's death, I knew that peace was one thing he would not claim to have laid hold of. He was content with our way of life. He loved Dakota and me. He didn't have many worries over the business. It was successful and enjoyable to maintain. Our lifestyle and the place where we lived were both about as peaceful as they could get.

And yet Dad rarely slept well. He suffered frequent headaches. He minded his own business and expected people to leave him alone with his, only allowing people so near and pulling back if they tried to dig deeper.

Except for the man beside me.

Dad had let Pastor Adams in. He'd read the entire Bible for the man!

I didn't know why and I suspected I'd never guess, but I supposed I should be thanking him instead of lashing out at him for harping on the God-stuff. He was a pastor. It was his job to harp on the God-stuff. And Dad had brought it up himself. Maybe in the hope of dealing with that need Pastor Adams had mentioned? That need that was always there though we liked to pretend it wasn't.

"I just don't like to see him hurting," I said quietly. It was more than the truth. It was my way of apologizing. I felt fairly confident that Pastor Adams would recognize it as such.

He seemed to. "I understand."

"You won't tell him I got on your case, will you?"

"Not a word," he said, "though I imagine he'd be proud to know you cared enough about him to speak up."

"Proud is not what he would be," I assured him.

Pastor Adams landed his fish—a nice sized brook trout—and put it mercifully out of its misery by smacking its head against the rock. Then he attached it to our stringer. "How many do you suppose we'll want?"

"As many as we can get," I said, thankful for the changed direction of our conversation and relieved that I hadn't offended

Pastor Adams. "We even endure the extra weight of squeeze butter to fry them in."

"Such sacrifices for your customers," he teased. "I'm humbled."

"Hey," I said, "you pick up that pretty yellow squeeze bottle of soft butter in the grocery store and drop it in the cart and it's nothing. But in your pack for thirty miles on top of your clothes, the ten to twelve packets of food you *do* need, the can of hot chocolate, snack bars, an extra tent, your sleeping bag and your roll-up mat, a few bottles of white fuel, your eating gear and half of the cooking gear, your flashlight, your insect repellent and sunscreen and biodegradable soap, your toilet paper, your matches, your water purification tablets and your water filter and your canteen, a shovel, a towel, your knife, the map, your fishing pole and lures and stuff, your rain gear, rope for the cooking tarp, a hammock, a first aid kit with enough junk in it for fifteen people, your baseball cap, your toothbrush . . ." I shrugged and pulled in an exaggerated breath. "That innocent looking container of squeeze butter can make the difference between an enjoyable trip and sheer torture. Especially at ten thousand feet."

"Ah," said the pastor as he reeled in a second brookie, "but it's worth it come day five or six."

"You bet it is," I said. "It'll be worth it tonight when we don't have to listen to Sophie complain about only having rice pilaf to eat."

"What if she doesn't like trout?" He grinned.

That possibility had not occurred to me. "We've never had someone not like it," I said. "Let's hope Dad sleeps through dinner just in case."

But Dad didn't sleep through dinner.

And Sophie did not like the trout.

It had been our experience in leading these hiking adventures that people would stay up past dark on the first night no matter how exhausted they were. There was just something about sitting around a campfire. Something about the night sky. Something about the warmth and light and security of nearness to the fire (and Dad's handgun) in contrast to the huge darkness of the wilderness all around . . . and the large and hungry animals that might be hiding there.

"What should we do if we hear a bear in camp?" Mrs. Sullivan asked my father as she kicked a half burned stick further into the fire. "Climb a tree?"

"That works with grizzlies," Dad said, "as long as it's a tree they can't push over. Black bears can climb trees. Remember that, just in case." He paused. "But no bears should come near camp tonight. We hung all the packs in trees downwind of us and none of you will be bringing food into your tents."

"But what if they do?" she persisted.

"Lie still. Don't panic. If they actually attack, curl up and protect your neck with your hands." He paused for a moment. "I'll hear if that happens and I'll take care of it. You just play dead and protect your neck until I do."

"What will you do?" Sophie wanted to know. Her tone was skeptical. Belittling.

"I'll attempt to scare it away or lure it to myself," Dad said. "I may have to spray it with pepper spray, in which case, if it's still near you, you'll get the experience of a lifetime." He picked up a thick branch and snapped a few twigs off to tuck them under the larger logs at the bottom of the fire. The wood was wet, so he was continually feeding in small pieces to keep the big pieces burning. "If worse comes to worst," he finished, "I'll shoot it."

"You guys are scaring me," Candice said. "Let's tell ghost stories instead."

"We will teach German song," one of the guys from Germany said.

So we learned a German song.

The newlyweds were the first to grab their flashlight and head to their tent. Mr. and Mrs. Sullivan followed shortly after them, as did the girls, the two men from Germany, Dakota, and Pastor Adams.

For a long time, probably almost an hour, the five of us remaining near the fire did not talk. But then the wind shifted and Neil D'Ary moved closer to me to get out of the path of the smoke and sparks that had begun to blow straight at his face.

"That's harsh," he said.

"I know it."

"How can you sleep up here knowing there are bears around?" he asked me.

I laughed. "You people sure are obsessed with bears."

"Well, you know, getting eaten could really put a kink in a person's vacation."

I hadn't intended to embarrass him. It was only natural for first-timers in the mountains to be frightened by the prospect of waking up to a snout in the face. They'd heard the stories of photographers and campers being mauled to death in the middle of the night for no apparent reason. They'd seen the footage of survivors. Their scars. They'd heard Dad insist more than once that nobody was going to bring food into their tent.

Still, I couldn't resist teasing him a little. "Oh, they rarely eat you." Then I laughed. "Neil," I said seriously, "we've been coming up here for six years, and we've only had that one bear incident that I told you about last night. They are typically as frightened of us as we are of them."

"What about wolves?" Ezra asked. "I heard that they haven't exactly been respecting the boundaries of Yellowstone Park."

"No," Dad said. "They haven't been. I'd be a lot more concerned if I heard a wolf howl in the middle of the night than if I saw a bear in camp because wolves travel in packs. One bear I can handle. A pack of wolves?" He shrugged. "Who knows."

"You aren't being a little too sure of yourself there, are you, Hayd?" Mr. D'Ary asked. "One bear you can handle." He laughed. "That I'd like to see."

What was it with people and their need to hurl insults at my father? It didn't happen so much during his hunting excursions or our shorter hikes and drives, but these long hikes seemed always to inspire it from one hiker or another. True, Dad wasn't the bubbliest of individuals, but he wasn't being paid to win any popularity contests. He was being paid to know where and where not to go—which he did. He was being paid to provide all the necessary equipment—which he did. He was being paid to keep everyone safe—which, barring that one bear attack that never would have happened if that woman had heeded his instructions, he did. What were people expecting anyway? Some naturalist guy in khaki shorts and sandal-hikers with a walking stick with bells on it who'd point out all the various flora and fauna?

"I would do whatever it took to keep my kids and my hikers safe," Dad told Mr. D'Ary. "That's what you'll see if anything comes up."

"He's done it before," Neil said.

"Don't I feel safe." Mr. D'Ary stood and stepped backwards over the chunk of wood he'd been sitting on. "Let's say goodnight, Neil."

Neil stood, said, "Yes, sir," but then sat back down. "Actually, I think I'll stay up."

"You need your sleep. Being up here doesn't change that."

"I'm not tired."

"I'm turning in and so are you."

"Relax, Dad," Neil said. "I'm not going to break any bones sitting out here by the fire and all the nasty little bees have gone to bed for the night."

"You can joke about it all you want," Mr. D'Ary said sternly, "but your health is nothing to play around with."

"Yeah, yeah. Wouldn't want to risk not winning one more trophy." Neil sighed when he stood up, but this time he did follow his father toward their tents.

I slid the chunk of wood Mr. D'Ary had been sitting on close to Dad and tried to make myself comfortable beside him. The night beyond the heat of the fire had turned cold and I had begun to shiver even though my face and the front of my pant legs were hot to the touch.

"Cold?"

I nodded and leaned in against Dad when he put his arm around my shoulders. "I don't know who to feel the most sorry for out of those two," I said quietly.

Dad squeezed me tightly against himself for a moment and then loosened his hold again. "You know the rule."

Yes. I knew the rule.

Keep to the trail.

"It's not your job or your place to feel sorry for either one of them," Dad said. "We get them over the trail. That's it. That's what we think about. That's what we do. That's where it ends."

"They've both got issues," Ezra said.

I nodded. "That's for sure."

Even though Dad thumped me lightly on the back of the head with one of his knuckles to let me know I was pushing his tolerance, he said, "Pastor Adams would say that they're both needy inside."

"Everyone is needy in his universe, Dad."

Ezra squinted at me from the other side of the flames.

"Would you say that we're not?" Dad asked me. "Needy?"

I turned back to him. "Us specifically?"

"No. Us in general. People."

"No." I pulled the cuffs of my jacket sleeves down over my hands. "I think we are pretty needy. I'm just not sure that what Pastor Adams gives as the panacea to that need is really the answer."

"I'm right there with you," Dad said.

"It's like this," Ezra said. "God created us to be able to know Him. We don't, for the most part, because mankind as a whole has gotten sidetracked. But each of us still has that basic longing inside. That's how He made us. It's like a puzzle piece in our psyche. We try to patch it with all kinds of junk, but the only thing that really fits in there is knowing God."

I leaned forward with my elbows on my knees and stared through the tops of the flames at Ezra. It was one thing to hear God-talk like that from an adult, a pastor. But Ezra was neither. He was a teenager. Only a year or two older than me. Pastor Adams had gone to bed and wasn't around for Ezra to please or appease. So why was he pouring on the piety?

"You really believe that." Dad said. It was an observation, not a question.

Ezra nodded. "I didn't always, though."

"Even though your father's a pastor?"

He laughed. "It's no different than anything else," he said. "Your job only rubs off so far on your kids and beyond that they're on their own."

"Like me not actually being a trail guide even though I go along with you all the time," I said to Dad.

"Right," Ezra said. "See, Mr. Craig, Jacy won't be a trail guide until she guides for herself. Without you. That's when you'll know if everything she's learned is really part of her or not."

"But God is more than just a job to your father," Dad said. "I have no expectation of Jacy spending her life doing what I do, but I'm sure your dad wants and expects you to share his faith."

"Yeah, he does. Still, nobody's a Christian because they were raised that way. Even pastors' kids. People become Christians when they accept Christ for themselves." Ezra stood up and stepped away from the fire. "I didn't do that until last year."

"Last year?" Dad seemed surprised.

"Yes, sir."

After a while I began to feel too warm. When Ezra began to head to his tent, I stood too and moved away from Dad to lie down on the dirt a few feet back from the fire. The piece of log I'd been sitting on was too thick to use as a "pillow" so I folded my arms behind my head. Dad and I didn't talk. We didn't have to. I watched the sparks and smoke rise up toward the stars. The campsite went completely quiet while I lay there except for the cracking and popping of the fire and Dad occasionally repositioning the wood. I rolled onto my side eventually and shut my eyes, and was only vaguely aware later of my sleeping bag being placed on top of me and of Dad rolling his out beside mine and getting inside it. The knowledge that I should open my eyes and crawl into my sleeping bag and zip it shut around me—the fire would die down before morning—presented itself to my half-asleep mind, but I dismissed it. I was perfectly comfortable where I was. Between Dad and the fire. Warm. Safe.

Until a scream displaced the quiet.

Dad was up and on his feet before I'd even lifted my head enough to see that the fire had burned itself down to glowing coals.

What time was it, I wondered.

But I didn't take the time to worry about it.

Dad was asking me where he'd set his flashlight.

"Next to the woodpile."

"Got it." He clicked it on and ran toward the noise.

I followed him.

"What's going on?" someone muttered from inside one of the tents as I passed by it.

"We're not sure yet," I said. "Stay put unless we tell you to do something else, okay?"

"Okay."

Dad shone his light on the Sullivan girls' tent where all the screaming was coming from. Nothing. He flashed the beam back and forth across the trees behind the tent. Nothing. Along the ground between the tent and us. Nothing.

"Something was chewing something right next to my head!" one of the girls yelled. She had abandoned all self-control and was thrashing about wildly inside the tent.

"Branches?" I asked Dad.

He shook his head. "Too high to reach their tent."

"Sophie!" Mrs. Sullivan screamed from inside her tent. "Candice?"

"Stay in your tent," Dad ordered.

"But—"

"I don't smell anything," I said above Mrs. Sullivan's protest. Grizzly bears had a very distinct and nasty scent.

"There's no bear," Dad said to me. Then louder, he said it again.

"Bear?" someone screamed from one of the other tents. "Did someone say *bear*?"

"There's no bear," Dad repeated. "Stay in your tent."

"If there's no bear," Mr. Sullivan mumbled, "what's everyone screaming about?"

I might have laughed if my system had not pumped itself so full of adrenaline. The "fight or flight" thing. I stayed alert and on edge as I followed my father right up to the girls' tent.

"It was going to eat me!" the screamer kept saying. Over and over again.

"Calm down." Dad stepped over one of the stake heads and set his foot down to a flurry of frantic noise. Between the rainfly and the tent. He shone his light down just in time for it to frame a porcupine making its terrified escape, quills all up and nose low to the ground. Dad took in and let out a long tense breath before informing whichever Sullivan girl was screaming that it had only been a porcupine.

Every muscle in my body relaxed as I shook my head and laughed nervously.

A porcupine.

What a relief.

"He ate some of your boot," Dad said as he dropped the boot on the ground in front of the tent.

"He was going to eat me!"

I stood back and watched in an undecided mixture of amusement and frustration as the tent flap was yanked open from the inside to let out a stumbling, stuttering, still screaming Sophie.

"It was going to eat me!"

"Sophie, get a grip," her father scolded from his tent. "Didn't you hear Mr. Craig? It was a porcupine. Porcupines don't eat people."

But Sophie was beyond reasoning with. She was terrified. Panicked out of her mind.

As always, Dad knew exactly what to do. He approached Sophie slowly with his hands held out in front of him until he was close enough to touch her, and then he placed his hands on her shoulders. "Sophie," he said calmly, "you're okay. You aren't hurt. Nobody else is hurt. It wasn't a bear. It's gone."

Sophie stopped screaming and started crying. "I thought . . . I thought it—"

"It's all right," Dad said.

Mr. and Mrs. Sullivan emerged from their tent and attempted to take over with Sophie, but Dad whispered them away. "Sophie," he said, "I want you to go back in your tent, get in your sleeping bag, and catch your breath." He kept looking straight at her as he pulled his hands away from her shoulders. "I'm going to stay right outside your tent to make sure nothing comes back around. Okay?"

Sophie was still shaking, but she managed a nod for my father and then turned and crawled back inside her tent.

"Candice," Dad said, "make plenty of room for your sister. Keep her away from the side of the tent."

"Yes, sir," Candice said.

"I'm sorry about that," Mr. Sullivan said to Dad and me. He sounded uneasy. Flustered. "She can be a bit dramatic."

Mrs. Sullivan nodded.

"She was scared," Dad said. "It happens."

"It was scary, Keith," Mrs. Sullivan said, nodding again.

"Yeah, well . . ." Mr. Sullivan pressed his hands to the bottoms of his coat pockets. "You can go back to your tent, Mr. Craig. I'll stay out here."

Dad rocked back on his heels and lifted his arm to press at the back of his neck. "Nope," he said. "I told her I'd be out here."

Mr. Sullivan rocked back on *his* heels. "She's my daughter."

"Sit out here with me if you want."

"You might as well get some sleep, Mr. Sullivan," I said. "Tomorrow is a lot of uphill."

Dad lowered himself stiffly to the dirt and rested his elbows on his knees. "Past timberline." He turned his face toward his shoulder to cough before holding his flashlight out to me. "Grab my jacket for me?"

"You bet."

Dakota was sound asleep when I got back to our tent and found Dad's jacket on the floor just inside the door. He could sleep through anything! Smiling, I zipped the flap shut and walked quietly and quickly back to where Dad was. Mr. and Mrs. Sullivan had retreated into their tent where I could hear them mumbling. I couldn't hear anything from the girls' tent.

"Do you think the porcupine will come back?"

"Yeah." Dad slipped his jacket on over his sweatshirt and snapped up all the buttons. "Fire's out, Jace. It's cold. Sleep in the tent."

I knew that I needn't worry about Dad being alone outside or being able to keep awake. And I knew that a porcupine was nothing to worry about anyway. Yet turning myself away from him and going back to our tent, even though it was what he'd asked me to do, levied every ounce of my will.

Was it because I was afraid? I didn't think so. I didn't *feel* frightened.

Maybe I was concerned for my father even though I knew I had no reason to be? Because I knew he still had his headache and probably needed a good night's sleep more than anyone else on this mountain?

No.

Whatever it was, it clung to me like a cat clawed to a screen.

And that unnerved me.

I wasn't used to apprehensions that I couldn't classify and file away.

CHAPTER 07

The trail posed less of a challenge than the overall mood of the hikers the next day, and there was nothing easy about the stretch of earth between Russell Lake and Fossil Lake. Lots of uphill. Lots of switchbacks. Lots of uneven ground, some of it nothing but fields of grapefruit-sized rocks. We walked through creeks and along mossy terraces. The bugs, millions of them, were relentless. Mosquitoes. Dragonflies. Horseflies. Deer flies. And once we'd pressed past timberline onto the open meadows and rocky fields of the plateau, the heat and the glare and the brightness of the sun badgered us.

Every step seemed to require more and more oxygen while the thinner air provided less and less of it. We were hot, tired, sore, weary of the weight on our backs, and not sure whether the spots we were seeing before our eyes were due to oxygen deprivation or the constant glare of the sun off all the bright white rocks and all throughout the close and merciless sky.

But those things were a normal part of the experience.

Testing the limits of body and mind and all that.

Thick moods, however, were not typical, and I wasn't sure how to handle them.

Dad wasn't moody, exactly, but he was sleep-deprived. Quiet.

Sophie was embarrassed.

Mr. Sullivan was peeved because of the way Dad had dismissed him and his wife during Sophie's little crisis.

The newlyweds had had some kind of tragic disagreement about which set of parents they'd share their first Christmas with since her parents lived in New Jersey and his lived in Arizona and they couldn't possibly visit both, so they were pouting.

Neil and his father were being even more hypercritical of one another than usual.

The two men from Germany had tired of all the ill-humored people around them and were developing their own cases of testiness.

So was Dakota.

The only happy people among us were Pastor Adams and Ezra, and their contentment seemed only to further annoy everyone else.

I had hoped that our stop for lunch at the murky green mineral lake underneath Bald Knob would refresh those who needed refreshing, but it didn't. Neither did our small breather at the Continental Divide. We stopped there to take pictures of our hikers adding their own rock to the ever-growing Can-You-Believe-How-Many-(or-how-few)-People-Have-Been-Here? Pillar that someone had decided to erect at the spot. This generated a few smiles, but only for the sake of snapping the pictures.

I'd often wondered why people considered it noteworthy, stepping over the Divide. It wasn't as if the spot on the trail was any more challenging or beautiful than any other—though it was beautiful. And it wasn't as if it made any actual difference to a hiker that water on one side of the imaginary line she was standing on would flow toward the Pacific Ocean while water on the other side would eventually find its way to the Atlantic. Yet every hiker that crossed this trail observed the spot. We always did, although Dad, Dakota, and I no longer put stones on the rock pillar.

When we started out again, I decided I'd walk with Dad. Fatigue, at least, was a state of being I could understand and empathize with. "How're you doing?" I asked him right off.

"I'm okay."

"Hot today," I said.

"Yep."

"Bright."

"Uh-huh."

If I was going to expend my breath, it wasn't going to be to talk about the weather. But since I couldn't think of anything else to talk about, I walked silently behind Dad for the next half mile listening to the sounds of our feet on the hard earth, our blue and white specked plates, cups, and silverware jostling around in our packs, the rhythmic squealing of the pack frames, water sloshing in Dad's plastic canteen, and to the wind.

Finally Dad said something. Something I almost didn't catch because he'd said it so quietly.

"I miss your mom, Jace."

He'd never said that aloud before. Ever. I suspected that he rarely allowed himself to acknowledge it in words even in the privacy of his own mind. But I knew he felt it. All the time.

"Do you?" he asked me.

The truth was that I'd grown so used to life without Mom since being seven that I couldn't say that I missed *her,* specifically, the person. I really couldn't even remember what she'd looked like when she wasn't smiling for a picture, though I did remember her voice. I did know that I had loved her and that I'd been terrified when she'd died and worried about where she'd go because she couldn't just be *gone.*

But that wasn't what Dad had asked me.

I supposed that in some ways I was missing having a mother. Someone to bake cookies with. Someone to help me explore my more feminine emotions, tastes, and concerns. Someone who wouldn't say "You know the rule" whenever I thought one of the guys on a particular trip was interesting. Someone who wouldn't be fearful of my transition from little girl to woman.

"I'm sorry, Jacy," Dad said.

My failure to answer right away must have intimidated him. "It's okay," I assured him. "I'm just . . . the question surprised me is all." I left it at that and hoped Dad wouldn't notice that I hadn't answered. I didn't know that he would understand. It might sound awful to him.

"Yeah," he said. "I'm sure it did."

"My guess would be that Pastor Adams has been telling you it'll help you deal with that need inside if you talk about Mom instead of pretending all the time that you don't hurt?"

He laughed quietly. "Sounds like I'm not the only one Bruce has been talking to."

"Actually," I confessed, "I talked to him." After giving Dad a summary of the conversation Pastor Adams and I had had, I said, "So is it helping? Thinking about Mom? Usually it only gives you a headache."

"It's done that, all right," he said. "I was thinking about how your mom loved this part of this trail. Up here above the trees. I was remembering actual conversations had up here. The wind blowing her hair." He let out a long breath. "No. It's not helping. How can it help to allow all those feelings in again only to be dragged back to the reality that I'm up here without her now?"

I didn't have an answer for him, so I said nothing.

He stopped walking on the trail and turned to face me. Pain tensed his features. The physical pain of his headache. The emotional pain of this raw hurt that at someone else's suggestion he'd dug at and now wished he hadn't. Like peeling off skin too soon after a severe sunburn.

But it had been eight years.

Dad should be able to remember Mom without it mangling his spirit like this.

Maybe Pastor Adams's suggestion did have merit. Maybe we could only learn to live with certain emotions by living with them. My father had not been living with his feelings about

Mom's death. He'd been living in spite of them. Living to stay ahead of them. In control of them. In denial of them.

I decided to take a risk. "Dad," I said carefully, "I really don't remember Mom. I mean, we don't talk about her and I was little when . . ."

"I know."

"Will you tell me about her? You know, the little things like what her favorite color was and where she would have gone if she could have gone anywhere."

"I . . ." He looked stunned. Exposed. But he reined all that in right there in front of me. His eyes showed the strain of the process. Then he nodded. "All right."

So as we walked the rest of the way to Fossil Lake, my father talked and I learned. I learned that my mother had played the violin . . . actually, I *remembered* that now that Dad had mentioned it. I learned that she had enjoyed quilting . . . come to think of it, I remembered *that* too. Her favorite color had been peach when she and Dad had first married, but she'd later taken a liking to ivory. I learned that she'd never learned to make fried chicken, which had intimidated her because Dad's mother made the best fried chicken on the planet.

That was true. Nobody made fried chicken like my Grandma Craig.

Dad recited a poem Mom had written when I was born and sang the little rhyme they'd made up for Dakota when he came along.

It was difficult for him. His words came slowly and quietly between a lot of pauses and an excessive number of reaches into his pocket for his handkerchief. His pace had become so quick that I knew we'd arrive at the lake a good hour before everyone else.

But that didn't matter. Dakota was back there with the hikers. Pastor Adams, too.

When we could see the lake and had both dropped our packs against a boulder at the foot of the meadow where we always made camp, I pointed at a blue speck on the other side of the water. A tent. The shoreline looked vacant other than that.

"Not a lot of other people on the trail this week," I said to Dad. We'd seen one group going back down toward Kersey Lake on horses, two guys from the FWP (the Department of Fish, Wildlife, and Parks), and one solo hiker who'd passed by us at Bald Knob who said he planned to hike beyond Fossil Lake to Dewey Lake for the night. Usually the trail was fairly populated up to Fossil Lake and then not again until Elk Lake five miles from the bottom on the other end. People liked to hike in from one end or the other and hike back out the same way if they only had a couple of days. And some people hiked the trail all the way through the other way from East Rosebud to Cooke Pass. But there was a lot more steep and demanding uphill right at the beginning coming from that direction, so Dad preferred to take beginners across starting at Cooke Pass. Then the last day, no matter what had happened in between, would be easy. Downhill. Plenty of trees. A roaring creek all along.

A good experience on which to begin a memory.

Fossil Lake was one of my favorite places on the trail because of its unique, almost otherworldly, terrain. It sat in sort of a bowl at the top of the plateau, so there was no view of the surrounding mountains except for a couple of peaks off in the distance. The lake was well above timberline but there were scrubby little bushes around. The ground was hard, grassy, rocky. The lake itself from above probably looked like a giant paint splotch with little dribbles spreading away at every angle. That's what it looked like on the map. I'd never walked the entire shoreline and didn't want to. It probably added up to miles and miles around all the little inlets and peninsulas and rocky outcroppings. The air always felt cold at this lake because of the ever-roaring wind even as the unobstructed sun burned down hot.

My favorite thing to do after helping Dad and Dakota set up camp and collect enough firewood for the night and morning was to walk several yards beyond camp to one particular massive but fairly flat white rock that I'd discovered. It was perfectly situated out of the wind. I'd undo my boots, stretch out face down on the rock and soak in the warmth from the sun. I'd fallen asleep many times doing that.

I wondered if my father had ever done that.

Probably not.

Not since he'd started hiking the trail as a guide anyway.

"Hey, Dad," I said, "how long do you figure we've got till people start showing up?"

He smiled. "Plenty of time to get a good start on the firewood."

I walked toward him and grabbed his hand. "You really must learn to delegate." I led him over a few boulders and down into the small hollow where my rock was. "Trust me?" I asked him.

"Yeah." He laughed. "Don't tell me you're thinking this would be a great place to pitch a tent."

"No." I smiled. "But close. Lie down."

"Jace, we have work to—"

I held up my hand to hush him.

It took quite a bit of convincing, but Dad eventually yanked his boots off and lay down on the rock beside me. "It's wonderful," he said. "The rock is warm. The sun is warm."

"No wind," I added.

"I can't remember the last time I felt this tired," he said.

"Get some sleep." I sat up and began the task of retightening my boot laces. "I won't tell anyone where you are."

He shut his eyes and nodded. Without argument. Without giving me instructions about when to wake him. Without saying he shouldn't be letting me talk him into this. Without apology.

"You're exhausted, Dad," I said.

"Can't see why. I've stayed up all night before."

"Ah, you know," I joked, "it's that aging thing." More seriously, I suggested that he might be coming down with something and reminded him that a two-day-old headache could be taxing all on its own. Then I stood, stretched, and started walking back toward our packs. It felt good to be leaving Dad in such a peaceful spot. He'd get some rest. He'd feel stronger. He'd—

"Craig!" a shout came up from the trail. It sounded like Mr. D'Ary. "Where are you, Craig? Neil's hurt himself!"

Dad squeezed my shoulder as he ran by me carrying his boots.

CHAPTER 08

"How's that?"

Neil tested the give in the bandage that Dad had wrapped around his wrist and nodded. "Good, sir. Thank you."

"You don't think it's broken?"

Dad looked up at Mr. D'Ary and shook his head. "I mean, I can't guarantee it, but he can move his fingers and nothing looks out of place."

"But you're no doctor."

"Right."

"It's not broken, Dad," Neil said. "It was tender anyway and I just aggravated it when I fell, that's all."

"Are you hurt anywhere else?" I asked Neil. I didn't want to stow away the first aid kit only to have to get it out again later.

He shook his head.

I snapped the lid shut more loudly than necessary and stomped off to put the kit back in my pack.

Neil got up and followed me. "I'm sorry," he said.

I spun around to face him and forced myself to smile. "Why would you be sorry, Neil? Anyone could trip on some of this ground."

"Yeah, but my father came up here screaming like I'd had a limb severed or something." He held his left wrist tightly against his body with his right hand. "You've got to be thinking I'm—"

This time my smile was genuine. "I'm not thinking anything," I said. "And even if I was, what matters is that you're okay. We've come far enough in now that it's a real pain to get out for help."

"I bet it is," he said.

"Speaking of pain . . ." I reopened the first aid kit and grabbed a couple of aspirin. "Take these." As we walked back toward our fathers, I asked, "So is your wrist the reason you're not playing tennis right now?"

"Yeah."

"It's probably kind of nice to have a break, huh?"

He nodded.

"That's one thing about what we do," I told him, "I never feel like I need a break."

"Most people probably think I shouldn't feel like that either," he said. "I'm just playing a game, right? How hard can that be? Traveling around, meeting famous people, talking to reporters, screaming fans." He shrugged. "Piece of cake, right?"

"I'm sure it's a lot of pressure," I said. "Especially . . ." My turn to shrug. Then I gestured toward his father.

"Right." He smiled, visibly relieved that I understood. "He takes all the fun out of it. All that matters is winning. The money. All I am to him is tennis. I mean I know he put a lot of money into getting me to where I've gotten and—"

"Neil," I said, "I'm sure he thinks he's doing what's best for you. That's what dads do."

"Not all dads," he said. "My father isn't like your dad."

Since that was obviously true, I didn't say it wasn't. "Well, you know, maybe now that you're eighteen you can kind of . . . I don't know . . . start . . ."

"Pulling away from him?" He laughed. "Jacy, the man is an octopus. He's got tentacles all over me. *I spent this much money. I gave up my own career. You owe it to your mother and me after all we've sacrificed to put you in a position to succeed. You'd be a loser on drugs if we hadn't pushed you all these years.*" He shook his head. "It goes on and on. All the time."

"Tell him you're going to be a loser on drugs if he doesn't back off." I smiled, but quickly squelched it because Neil stiffened. "I'm sorry, Neil."

When he waved my apology away as if it was some kind of foul odor, his green eyes went harsh. "I know, Jacy. I'm just a big sniveler." He shook his head. "You don't understand. Nobody understands." He turned quickly away from me and started running down the rocky slope toward the water.

"Where's he going?" Dad called to me.

"Neil!" Mr. D'Ary dropped the stack of tent stakes he'd been holding and ran by me after his son.

Dad came and stood beside me and both of us watched Mr. D'Ary stop on the shore in frustration when he couldn't catch up with Neil, who just kept running. "What happened?" Dad asked me.

"I . . . I didn't keep to the trail."

After I'd told Dad everything Neil had said to me and everything I'd said to him, he pulled me close for a moment and hugged me. "I'll go talk to him. Make sure he stays safe. He can't run forever. Not up here."

"I'm sorry, Dad."

"Hey," he said as he stepped away from me and lifted my chin with his hand, "this isn't your fault. This has been between them probably since Neil started showing promise on the tennis court. You just happened to be here to get in the middle of it."

"You're not mad at me?"

"No." He walked back with me to our packs and sat on a boulder to get into his boots again. When he'd finished lacing them up, he said, "Can't say for sure how long I'll be out there. Get the tents up for me? Fire going? Catch some fish?"

I nodded.

"Thanks."

As I unstrapped our tent from the top of Dad's pack, I watched him walk down the slope and speak to Mr. D'Ary. I couldn't hear what he was saying because of the distance, but I could see his face. He looked angry. Especially when, at one point, he looked and pointed up toward me.

I busied myself with setting up the tent, but I would have given anything to know what Dad had said. Especially when Mr. D'Ary rejoined me at the campsite and got to work on setting up his tent without a word to me, a complaint, or any questions.

Dakota, Pastor Adams, and the other hikers trickled their way into camp and we fell into the routine of late afternoon. Mr. and Mrs. Sullivan went into their tent for a nap. The two guys from Germany and the newlyweds—who'd apparently resolved their in-laws issue—went down to the lake to fish. Dakota collected and broke up the firewood. The two Sullivan girls sat on the grass to take turns brushing and rebraiding one another's hair.

Since Sophie was at the back brushing Candice's hair, I sat behind her and slowly removed the band at the bottom of her braid. She had beautiful thick long blond hair that actually held a braid without hairspray. My brown hair would never do that, which was one of the reasons I always kept it short. Long scraggly fly-away do-nothing hair would only get in the way up here. "Believe it or not," I said, "I can do a pretty decent French braid. Would you like one?"

"Okay," she said.

I held my hand out to her for their brush. "Are you doing okay?" I parted her hair.

She nodded.

"You have a choice," I said. "I can make one braid or one on each side. What do you think?"

"Whichever."

I decided to do two braids. It would give me more time to talk with her. And more time off my feet. "What did you think of the hike today?" I asked her. "Brutal?"

"Yeah."

"Would you ever have imagined you'd be able to do something like this?"

It took her a couple seconds to answer. "No."

"We're a lot stronger than we give ourselves credit for sometimes," I said.

"And sometimes," said Pastor Adams, who'd come up from the lake with a whole string of fish, "we're a lot weaker and it scares us."

I glared at him. Here I was, laboring to bolster Sophie's boldness for the night ahead, and he strolls up and makes a moronic comment like that?

To my surprise, though, Sophie said, "That's exactly how I felt last night." She apologized for moving and then settled into a still position again. "If that would have been a bear chewing on my boot right next to my head," she said to Pastor Adams, "I'd have been dead and there would have been nothing I could have done to stop it."

"Dad would have stopped it," I said.

"He would have tried," Pastor Adams agreed. "But as hard as your father works to be in control and keep things in control, Jacy—"

I shot him a warning glance. Preaching was one thing, and he was welcome to it. But tearing away at our hikers' confidence in Dad?

Bad business.

And stupid. If Sophie woke up screaming again we'd all have a bad night's sleep. One bad night's sleep on a trip like this was workable. Two could be potentially dangerous. Tired hikers tended to be less prudent.

"Dad's the best there is at what he does," I said.

Sophie nodded and then apologized for moving her head again.

"I'm not saying he's not," Pastor Adams said quietly. "If there's a man out there I'd count on to keep this kind of group safe for the next four days, it's him." His eyes softened as he stared directly at me. "But even your father has things he can't handle. A breaking point."

I had to look away from Pastor Adams. Back at Sophie's hair.

"He handled quite the hysterical idiot last night," Sophie said. She'd put on a less than serious tone, but her shoulders had tensed up slightly. "I'd say your Dad can handle just about anything, Jacy."

"He has his . . ." *Weakness.* ". . . things."

And sometimes we're a lot weaker and it scares us.

I finished Sophie's braids without more conversation, helped Dakota tie the rainfly down over the final tent, and then walked up a hillside in the hope of being able to see Dad and Neil D'Ary.

All I could see was dirt, rocks, that other tent across the lake, and the glare of the sun off the peaks of the waves. Thousands and thousands of points of blinding, wavering light.

Darkness settled in over the lake. Darkness and clouds.

"It's going to storm tonight," Dakota leaned toward me to whisper.

I glanced around the campfire at the faces on every side of it. We'd just finished dinner and everyone was wondering, though nobody would say it aloud, where Dad and Neil could be.

I stood up. "Let's, uh, get the packs put up." I allowed the wind to push at me for several moments and then pointed in the direction it was going. "There're no trees, but try to set them behind a ridge or something out of the wind. Pastor Adams, could you and Ezra bring a tarp and cover them? I think we're going to get some rain."

"Sure."

Thunder pounded the sky in the distance.

"Mr. D'Ary, you might want to pull a change of clothes out for Neil," I said. "In case it starts raining before they get back."

He nodded.

I disregarded the nervous fear that had made his nod jerky and unsure. "Dakota, get some clothes for Dad."

"Already on it," he said.

When Pastor Adams returned from covering the packs, he threw several large branches on the fire. "We'll need to keep this going even if it's raining," he said. "So they'll know where we are once it's dark." He glanced quickly around the campsite as he pulled his hood up and yanked the strings to tighten it. "Everyone in their tents?"

I nodded and then quietly, so nobody—especially Mr. D'Ary—would hear, said, "This isn't like Dad."

"You know how it is up here," he said. "You can go farther than you realized you were going." He pulled a stump right up to the fire and sat down on it. "And it always takes longer getting back."

"Yeah." That was true. "Because you're telling yourself the whole time that you're sure you never came this far."

He laughed. "Been there."

Still, I couldn't help trying to remember what both Neil and Dad had been wearing when they'd left. Neil had on jeans and a black sweatshirt. Dad had on jeans and one of his red T-shirts with our logo on the front pocket. Neil would be warmer than Dad, but neither of them would be warm enough. It got cold at this elevation at night. Most often down to thirty-five degrees or lower. It had snowed on us more than once at Fossil Lake. And if it rained, that would make the cold feel even colder and . . .

I shook my head and forced myself to look at Pastor Adams. Worrying would only make the waiting worse, and it wouldn't help Dad and Neil anyway. "Maybe you could go talk to Mr. D'Ary," I said. "I think he's pretty scared."

Pastor Adams nodded and stood up. "If that's what you want me to do."

"You're a pastor," I said nervously. "You're bound to be better at the comforting business than I am."

"Especially since it's your father out there too?"

I looked at the flames. "Yeah."

"All right. I'll go talk to him and be back out."

While Pastor Adams was inside Mr. D'Ary's tent, it began to rain. One drop at a time at first. Big heavy drops. But all too soon it started dumping down in sheets, bulldozed forward and out by the wind. Lightning hit. Thunder roared.

I wasn't afraid of the storm. I loved storms in the mountains. I didn't necessarily like sitting outside in them though, and I was having a hard time keeping the fire burning.

I stretched my rain poncho over my knees and bent to shove more twigs into the fire. Even though the plastic of the poncho was keeping me dry, it was useless when it came to keeping out the cold of the water hitting it. But I had layered three different shirts underneath it, including a thermal long john shirt, so I did stay warm.

Dakota and Ezra joined me next to the fire. Ezra sat beside me while Dakota got down on his hands and knees to blow steadily into the bottoms of the struggling flames. Pastor Adams rearranged the burning sticks a bit when he returned, but even that didn't help. The rain was just too overpowering.

Lightning hit again. Nearby. It shook the ground. Booming. Close. All around. Everywhere. And why shouldn't it feel, sound, and be like that? We were right up in the storm. With nothing to muffle its force.

"I think I see them!" Pastor Adams shouted over the wind after a white hot flash of lightning. "Just for a second," he stood and said, "I saw red."

Dakota, Ezra, and I got to our feet and watched the darkness in the direction Dad and Neil had gone, waiting for another lightning flash.

One came. Then another.

Then I saw them!

It was strange, the way they appeared to shimmy back to camp in the bright and wildly variable flashes of silver light. Like images from some kind of strobing computer game.

"They're still a long ways off," Ezra said. "They're going to be cold."

Frustration tightened my fists as I glanced down at our pathetic fire. "This'll never warm them up," I said. "The rain is killing it."

Pastor Adams nodded. "The best thing for them to do anyway is get right in their tents, into dry clothes, and into their sleeping bags."

For a half hour with absolutely no break in the weather, we watched Dad and Neil get closer and closer to us in the increasingly frequent flashes of lighting.

"Your God wouldn't find it entertaining to strike one of us, would He?" I jokingly asked Pastor Adams since, standing, we were the high points in the basin and there were no trees.

"No," he replied without humor, "He wouldn't."

He'd barely gotten the last word out when a huge flash ignited the sky right above the lake in violent and ripping noise. And then it hit the water. A taste like aluminum dried out my mouth and cold sweat broke on the back of my neck and above my upper lip. Dakota, Ezra, Pastor Adams, and I stumbled to the ground in the same instant, and I could see in the next flash of lightning that Dad and Neil had done the same.

"Boiled fish, anyone?" Dakota shouted over the noise of the downpour.

For the next few minutes none of us dared to move. The rain turned to hail and pelted us with square little pea to marble sized chunks. Then it softened to rain again as the fury of the storm rolled on to batter another part of the mountain.

I got to my feet and ran to Dad when I saw him and Neil coming toward us again. Both of them were drenched, soaked through. Shivering. I grabbed Dad's arm while Pastor Adams grabbed Neil's and we led them back to camp where Dakota helped Dad get settled in our tent and Mr. D'Ary took Neil inside his.

Pastor Adams waited with me until Dakota poked his head out of our tent door to tell me that Dad had changed and I could come in whenever I wanted.

"Good night," I said to Pastor Adams. "Thanks for all your help tonight when Dad was gone."

"Anytime."

I laughed. "Actually, never again would suit me just fine."

"Me too," he said. "Go look after your dad. Ezra and I will go see how the D'Arys are doing before we head over to our tent."

I hurried into our tent and pulled off my wet boots and rain poncho. Before crawling into my sleeping bag, I leaned over Dad and placed my hand against his face.

Cold.

His hand found mine and held it tightly, but his shivering prevented his being able to say anything.

So I talked to him. I told him how the evening had gone. I told him that Sophie had seemed fine tonight. That she hadn't even asked me if porcupines ventured up this high. I told him how much of a help Pastor Adams had been to me in the practical tasks of setting up camp and preparing dinner as well as with Mr. D'Ary.

I didn't tell him how deeply his absence had unnerved and frightened me.

Nor did I tell him that I'd made a joke about God striking us with lightning.

Nothing about that seemed funny anymore.

CHAPTER 10

When the morning sun began to brighten the inside of our tent in the sea blue color of our rainfly, I wasn't surprised to roll onto my side and find Dad's sleeping bag already stowed in its red sack at my feet. I'd awakened several times during the night to check on him, and he'd been awake each time. He'd never really warmed up either. Not fully.

I mumbled a warning to Dakota to keep his face turned and then quickly changed into clean clothes inside my sleeping bag. I slipped my boots on but didn't tie them and made my way out of the tent.

Dad ladled some boiling water from the kettle he'd hung over the fire into my cup when I held it out to him, and I stirred in a spoonful of instant hot chocolate.

For a few minutes I stood behind Dad, shifting my weight from foot to foot and sipping my hot chocolate, trying to warm up. Morning air was crisp, clear . . . and cold.

"How are you feeling?" I asked Dad after a while even though I was disinclined to because I knew he'd say "okay" even if he felt awful.

"I'm okay," he mumbled into his own cup of hot chocolate.

I pulled up a rock and sat beside him. "What happened last night, Dad? Why were you so late getting back?"

He stared at the steam rising from his cup. "I misjudged how far we'd gone."

"That's what we were thinking," I said. "Did you get to talk to Neil at all?"

"For hours."

I elbowed him. "You know what I mean."

"Yeah. I talked to him."

"And?"

"And I'll be happy when this trail is safely behind us."

Something about his tone concerned me. "What do you mean?"

For the first time that morning he looked straight at me. "His cylinders are firing pretty unpredictably right now, Jace. And he's feeling hopeless. Not a good combination."

I nodded.

"Will you help me see to it that one of us is always near him?"

"Sure. But you don't think . . ."

"I don't think I can afford not to think of every possibility."

"It's amazing, isn't it?" I added more water to my cup. I'd put in a little too much chocolate mix. Too sweet. "From far away Neil looks like a guy who's got everything going for him. I mean, he's made lots of money and is on the way to making a whole bunch more. He's famous. He's great-looking. He's—"

"You think so, do you?" Dad asked.

"Yes."

"Hm," he said.

Heat rose in my cheeks, and I had to labor to keep a stupid grin off my face. "What I was saying, Dad, is that he's successful as far as anyone can define it and yet he's miserable."

The fire sizzled when Dad tossed another still-wet branch onto it. "Some people are never happy."

"You think that's all it is?" What was the word Neil had used? "You think he's just a *sniveler*?"

"It's not my place to think anything."

I sighed. Once those words had come out of Dad's mouth, the conversation was over. Finished. Even if I kept talking. I set my cup down on the dirt and stood up. "Stay warm by the fire," I told him. "I'll take care of breakfast."

He smiled up at me. "I might just take you up on that."

The walk down to where Ezra and Pastor Adams had secured our packs for the night was pleasant enough. The air smelled thick with wet dirt and wood. The grass looked even greener than it had the day before because of the moisture, and the lake looked even bluer because of the deep blue cloudless sky and the angle of the early sun. My boots slipped up and down over my ankles as I stepped carefully around rocks because I still hadn't tied them. I didn't mind the looseness of them, and I was careful not to trip over the long gold laces.

They'd be tied up tight soon enough.

Breakfast consisted of two granola bars and a packet of instant oatmeal for each of us. Dad liked to start out early and never wanted to bother too much about breakfast since taking down camp ate up a good chunk of time as it was. Especially when it had rained because we'd want to unstake the tents and move them around to allow the sun some time to dry them along with anything else that had gotten wet. Wet things weighed more than dry things, and the smell of a tent that had been rolled up wet and packed all day in its cinched-shut bag wasn't exactly inviting.

Pastor Adams and Ezra were the first to join Dad and me. The two men from Germany soon made their appearance. Once conversation and laughter started intruding on the silence of the morning, everyone got up and made their way to the fire for breakfast.

Nobody complained about the food.

"That was some storm last night," Mrs. Sullivan commented.

Dad nodded. Then he looked across the fire at Neil D'Ary. "Were you warm this morning?"

"No, sir."

Dad laughed. "I wasn't either. Fire'll help."

"Yes, sir." Neil sounded like a recording being played on a machine with low batteries.

"I have some instant coffee in my pack," I said. "I can make some for you, Neil."

He didn't even look at me. "Caffeine isn't part of my program."

Dad tapped the side of my leg with the top of his hand. "Go ahead and bring it."

So I made the walk back to my pack. Again.

Most of the hikers had left the fire to start packing up their sleeping bags and clearing their tents by the time I'd climbed back up over the hill and down into camp again. Dad grabbed the container of coffee from me, opened it, poured a scary amount of it into a cup, scooped in some water, stirred it, and held it out to Neil. Before speaking to Neil, though, he glanced quickly at Mr. D'Ary. His expression was as crystal clear as the water in Fossil Lake.

Don't mess with me.

Mr. D'Ary glared right back at Dad. But even as he did, he tossed what was left of his granola bar into the fire and got to his feet. "Do what Mr. Craig tells you to do, Neil," he said. Then he turned and walked over to his tent.

Neil accepted the coffee from Dad. "I guess that's one way to make yourself feel like you're in charge even when you're not and you know it."

"I'm in charge," Dad said. "Drink it."

"Yes, sir." Neil sounded more lively already.

But he still looked awful.

Breakable.

As soon as I finished my oatmeal, I lifted the kettle from the fire and set it on a rock to cool a little so we could use the warm water to rinse our dishes.

"Do you ever feel pressure up here?" Neil asked me when Dad left to help Dakota take down our tent.

I'd felt plenty of pressure the night before, being responsible for the campsite while Dad had been gone. But since that had happened because of Neil, I didn't say so. I just shrugged.

"I suppose your dad does all the time," he said.

"I don't think he looks at it as pressure," I told him. "He just does his job."

"But he's got to feel it," Neil said. "Taking people who don't know the first thing about camping way up here to the middle of nowhere? Someone could get lost or hurt or mauled." He shook his head and then grimaced when he took another sip of his coffee. "This stuff is stout."

"Just Dad's way of dealing with the pressure of having a potentially sleepwalking hiker on his hands."

Neil laughed and I was glad to hear it.

"Now I'm going to be bouncing off the walls," he said.

I smiled. "Nobody bounces at ten thousand feet."

The sun began to warm the air as we worked on packing up camp. It felt wonderful through my dark T-shirt, but it also revived millions of mosquitoes. I tried to keep moving as much as I could, helping the Sullivan girls roll up their tent and then hauling packs back up to the trail with Dad and Dakota.

As we headed away from camp for the third and final time, I thought I heard a shout coming from the direction of the lake. I raised my hand to still Dad and Dakota. They stopped instantly, and the three of us stood there listening. At the repeat of the sound I'd heard, which was unmistakably a shout, Dad, Dakota and I bolted back toward camp. A quick scan of the site from the top of the hill accounted for all twelve of our hikers, none of whom were shouting.

"There's that tent across the lake," Dakota said. "Do you suppose they're in trouble?"

"Let's go check it out," Dad said to him. To me he said, "Finish bringing up the packs and tell everyone what's up."

I didn't argue though the last thing I wanted to do was be left behind without Dad again. Without Dad *and* Dakota. Quickly, I recruited Pastor Adams to help me with the packs and explained to him that "anytime" had arrived.

He shielded his eyes with his hand and appraised the situation. "It'll take them about half an hour to get around to them," he said. "Let's get all the tents on the packs so we'll be ready to go as soon as they get back."

"What if someone's hurt over there?"

"Then," he said, "I imagine your father will come up with a plan."

That made me feel a little better.

But that feeling of well-being dissipated an hour and a half later when I saw Dad and Dakota coming back with two women. One of them had hold of Dakota's arm, and Dad was carrying the other in his arms.

My distress must have shown in my face because Pastor Adams said, "It doesn't look so bad. They're both conscious. Smiling, even."

I nodded. "If anyone was still hurt over there, Dad would have left Dakota."

"That's what I was thinking."

We all kept a decent distance when Dad and Dakota came into camp, and Dad found a spot in the shade of a boulder to gently set down the woman he'd been carrying.

"Everyone," he said, wiping sweat from his forehead with his forearm, "this is Cara Benoit and her niece, Emily." He sat in the dirt beside Cara Benoit and pointed at her left ankle, which had been heavily bandaged in what looked like a pink and white flannel shirt. "Cara got her foot caught between two rocks and broke her ankle real good."

I grimaced. *Ouch.*

But Cara Benoit looked remarkably composed and in possession of herself. "I don't know what we would have done if this had happened after you all had gone," she said to Dad.

"Someone would have been along," he said.

"Yeah." She smiled, and then tensed a little as her hand went instinctively to her ankle. "But when?"

"Well, we were still here," he said, "so no use worrying about that."

While they'd been talking, Dakota had escorted Emily to a spot close to her aunt and helped her sit down. Emily looked like she was about my age. Because of the way she'd allowed Dakota to lead her, the way she held her eyes only half open, and because Dakota told her things like *There's a rock right there* and *Your aunt is about three feet away from you to your left*, I deduced that she was blind. At least partially.

"What I'm going to do," Dad said as he got to his feet again, "is hike back a mile or so on the trail to that lake where we saw those FWP guys camped." He was looking steadily at Pastor Adams. "They'll probably have a radio. They can hike back up with me and stay with the ladies until help comes. It'll mean you all will be waiting here for another couple of hours, but I'm not comfortable with any of my other options at this point."

Pastor Adams nodded.

So did Dakota and I.

But one of the men from Germany had a different idea. "We can hike ahead?"

"No," Dad said.

"I do not pay to sit at lake."

70

"We'll still get out on schedule," Dad assured him. "We'll just have to skip the fishing stop today." He looked down at Cara Benoit and then at Emily. "It's not a big deal. It's what we do up here when someone needs help." He looked again at the man from Germany. "And it's what we hope someone would do for us if we ever found ourselves in trouble."

"Yes," the man said, nodding. "Of course you are right."

"I feel so stupid," Cara Benoit said.

"Don't." Dad knelt beside her again. "Jacy? Will you bring me the first aid kit? I already reset her ankle, but I need to wrap it properly."

I nodded and went to get it.

Tears came to Cara Benoit's eyes when Dad rewrapped her ankle, but she didn't utter a word of complaint. In fact, she thanked him when he finished. "Can I go with you?" I asked Dad when he handed me the first aid kit.

"No."

"Why not? I can keep up—"

"We're not going to argue about this, Jacy." He grabbed hold of my arm and led me away from everyone. "I need you here."

"Why?"

"We talked about that already."

I squinted at him, not understanding. Then I remembered. Neil D'Ary. "Dad, I can't—"

He held up his hand.

I shut my mouth.

"I'll be back by lunch time," he said.

I stared down at the dirt and nodded.

He touched my arm.

I pulled away.

"We'll talk later," he said. And then he left.

For a few minutes, I was angry with him. Furious. But then I piled reason over it like I'd shovel dirt over a still smoldering fire. Someone had to go for help, and Dad had yet to allow Dakota or me to hike alone. There were twelve hikers and two newcomers, one of whom was hurt and the other blind. It wouldn't have been right for Dad to dump all of that on Dakota, even with Pastor Adams there to help. And Neil D'Ary did seem to feel comfortable with me. More comfortable than with anyone else on the hike—with the possible exception of Dad.

Realistically, leaving me behind had been Dad's only reasonable course of action.

And he'd be back by lunch time.

While Pastor Adams took most of the hikers down to the lake to fish and Dakota played a game of cards with Neil D'Ary, I talked with Cara Benoit and Emily. Cara explained that she had taken Emily, her brother's daughter, on a trip of this kind each summer since Emily had been old enough to walk. A high school English teacher, Cara always had summers off and Emily had grown to love getting out and trying new things with her semi-adventurous aunt.

"You two must be more than semi-adventurous," I said, "hiking a trail like this on your own."

"I love to do things that everyone thinks blind people can't do," Emily told me.

"And I might get too old to do anything if I wait to do things until I meet my knight in shining armor," Cara said.

I couldn't imagine Cara Benoit having all that much trouble meeting men. She was beautiful. Thick brown hair. Vivid hazel eyes. Fit. And strong emotionally. It could be a matter of choosiness, I supposed. Or Cara could live in a small town where all the decent guys were already married or a lot older than her.

But I didn't ask her to elaborate.

Keep to the trail.

At noon Pastor Adams came up from the lake with his stringer of fish, and the two of us prepared lunch for everyone. Cara fell asleep after that, and the Sullivan girls and their parents took Emily for a walk down to the lake. Both guys from Germany paced around a bit but then decided to put up their tent again to catch a nap away from all the mosquitoes. The newlyweds ventured off on a short stroll. Pastor Adams told them to stay within sight of the lake at all times, and they promised they would. Neil D'Ary's caffeine had worn off and he'd fallen asleep on a flat gray rock in the sun with a fleece shirt thrown over his head to keep the mosquitoes off. And Mr. D'Ary sat in front of the fire and kept it burning even though the afternoon sun beat down hot and inescapable on the whole top of the mountain.

After helping Dakota and me get Cara settled in the center of her shade again after it had moved, Ezra asked me if I felt like fishing.

"No."

"It's a good thing we were still around this morning when Cara hurt herself," he said, "because nobody's 'been along' yet."

I nodded. I had noticed that too.

"It's getting late," he said.

"Sure is."

"I'm sure it's just that the FWP guys had already left the lake, and your dad has gone down the trail looking for them," he said.

"I'm sure you're right," I said.

But when dinner time had come and gone and we'd eaten and cleaned up and had put up all the tents again and there was still no sign of Dad, I felt sure of only one thing.

Something horrible had happened.

And the last thing between us had been me pulling away from him.

CHAPTER 11

"Don't act so scared."

I glared at my brother. We'd gone inside our tent to roll out our sleeping bags and grab warmer jackets and our flashlights. It was getting dark. "How should I act? I am scared."

"I know that," he said. "But you can't act like you are."

"They'll understand."

"What they'll do," he said, "is get scared."

I knew he was right. Dad wouldn't want us to panic. In fact, he'd expect us not to panic. "Okay," I said. "We'll tell them that Dad must have had to hike all the way out to find help on account of the trail being so slow this week."

"That's probably what happened," Dakota said.

"Yeah," I said. "Or he could have fallen or run into a bear or—"

"Jace, this is Dad we're talking about." He pulled his jacket over his head and zipped it to his chin. "From the bottom he's probably had time to hike at least halfway back up, which means he'll be here tomorrow by lunch time."

Why wasn't Dakota afraid, I wondered. I was terrified.

"If that is true, Dakota," I said, "he's going to be dead on his feet. And shouldn't the guys on horses or the helicopter or whatever have been here for Cara and Emily by—"

"Jacy! Dakota!" Pastor Adams tapped the side of our tent as he ran by it back toward the trail. "He's coming!"

Forgetting my warmer jacket and my flashlight, but remembering to rezip the tent flap out of force of habit, I followed Dakota outside and up the hill behind Pastor Adams.

Dad met us about halfway down and pulled me close to him first thing. He felt warm against me even though the perspiration on his arms and face had turned cold in the night air. He held me the whole time he explained to us that he'd had to hike nearly all the way to Kersey Lake before catching the FWP guys because they'd gone out as far as Russell Lake the previous night. "When I left them," he finished, "they were going to hike out to pick up a couple of horses and then ride in as far as they could get before dark. They'll head in to Fossil Lake first thing in the morning for Cara and Emily."

No wonder he was so warm. He'd just hiked a good twelve to thirteen miles. More, depending on how far he'd hiked off the trail to get down to those lakes where he thought he'd find the Fish and Game guys.

"Cara hasn't gotten any worse, has she?" he asked Pastor Adams.

"No. She's a trooper."

"They asked me if I figured she needed to be airlifted out of here, and I told them I didn't think so, . . . but then I worried about it all the way back up. You know, what if she started going into shock or something? I mean, she shouldn't because I'd reset the bone and she wasn't bleeding anyway and all but—"

Dakota grabbed Dad's arm and I stepped back from him.

He was rambling . . . and second guessing himself.

Two things he only did when he was ready-to-fall-over exhausted. I didn't think I'd ever seen him do both at the same time.

"She's fine," Pastor Adams assured him.

"Good. Okay. Good."

"Let's head over to the fire, Dad," Dakota said. "You must be starving."

"Actually," he said, "maybe just something hot to drink?"

"I'll get it," I told him.

So while Pastor Adams and Dakota walked with Dad toward the fire Mr. D'Ary was still overseeing, I walked back to our packs—yet again—and pulled out a pan to boil water in and one of our single-serving packets of instant soup.

I took a moment while I was at the packs to thank God that Dad had returned and that all my fearfulness had been for nothing. I thanked Him that all of us had stayed safe all day, especially Neil D'Ary. I thanked Him that help was on the way for Cara and Emily. And I asked Him to please divert the lightning and the porcupines tonight so that Dad could finally get some desperately needed sleep.

Then I scolded myself aloud. "If God is real, it probably really offends Him that I'm jabbering at Him now, since I never even think about Him when I'm not scared."

Somehow, though, I thought that God would understand. And at least when I had decided to talk to Him, it had been to express gratitude and not to promise Him I'd serve Him forever if He'd only convince Dad that I needed my own horse.

Before rejoining the others at the fire, I walked down to one of the streams flowing into the lake and filled the pan with water. My hands were nearly numb from holding onto the cold metal by the time I got up the slope and set the pan to heat. I sat beside Dad, who'd sat beside Cara Benoit, and squeezed my hands together between my knees.

"The pain's not too bad," Cara was telling Dad. "Of course your kids have kept me on a pretty steady supply of painkillers and have been keeping my ankle packed in a lake-soaked towel." She shivered. "That is some cold water, let me tell you."

"I'm really sorry I couldn't get you out of here today," Dad said.

She smiled and rested her hand on his arm. "It's not as if you didn't try."

Dad glanced down at her hand and then nervously over at me. He leaned back a little on the boulder he was sitting on and then gently yanked his arm free of Cara's hold to raise his hand to cover his mouth through a spurt of coughing. When he finished, he muttered something about the stupid smoke and then sat up straight with his arms tight against his body and his hands clasped on his lap.

But no smoke had blown toward Dad. I knew it, and so did Cara Benoit.

Apparently drawing the most obvious conclusion that she had unnerved my father, which clearly had not been her intention, Cara looked away from him at the flames.

Dad repositioned himself on his boulder. "How's that water coming?"

"Not quite boiling," I told him.

He grabbed my shoulder and pushed down on it as he got unsteadily to his feet. "You know what?" he said. "I'm starting to see double." He laughed. "I think I'm going to turn in." He said his good nights to the few of us who were still beside the fire and went straight to our tent.

"I'm sorry," Cara mouthed to me.

I waited until everyone but Dakota, Pastor Adams, Cara and I had left the fire for the night to acknowledge her apology. "He hasn't really gotten over Mom yet," I told her.

"Dakota told me she had died," Cara said. "I'm sorry."

"It was a long time ago. But . . . well . . . you're probably the first woman to touch Dad for any other reason than steadying herself on the trail since Mom." I smiled. "I mean, he's not exactly the let's-all-come-together-for-a-big-group-hug-before-you-go-home kind of guy."

"I've kind of gathered that," she said, laughing a little.

Dakota scooted closer to the fire. "You didn't do anything wrong, Cara. Dad's just—"

"Tired," Pastor Adams said.

"Tired," Dakota agreed.

But I had to wonder if it was really as simple as that.

"Well, he certainly has reason to be," Cara said. Then she looked at Pastor Adams. "So, what kind of church do you pastor?"

He told her.

"I just became a Christian," she said. "Last year. Emily too."

"Really?"

"Really."

And then it started. A whole hour's worth of God-talk.

I didn't mind it exactly. In fact I felt a bit envious of the way these two total strangers could immerse themselves in such enthusiastic and honest conversation about the things God had supposedly done in each of their lives.

Of course the whole of my life that I could remember had been spent with Dad, who avoided to the point of occasional rudeness conversation that ventured beyond the minutia of the trail. I had witnessed many animated and genuine conversations, but they had always happened between people who had come together on a particular trip. People who already knew one another.

Pastor Adams and Cara Benoit had not met before today and yet they seemed to feel completely at ease with one another. Like Dakota and me, almost. Or like Sophie and Candice.

I supposed that Pastor Adams or Cara would point out, if I mentioned my observation to them, that they *were* "brother" and "sister" in God's family, or something trite like that.

I decided not to give them the opportunity. Instead I stood to do some pointing out of my own. "It's getting late." I looked at Pastor Adams. "We should get Cara to her tent and get some sleep." Then I looked at Cara. "I don't imagine that all the jostling of riding a horse is going to feel so great on your ankle tomorrow."

She grimaced a little, but then said, "It's bound to feel better than trying to walk on it would."

"That's for sure," I agreed.

I shone the flashlight ahead of Dakota and Pastor Adams as they supported Cara Benoit across the rocky ground to her tent. Dakota handed her a couple of aspirin and said, "Call out if you need anything."

She smiled.

"Don't even think twice about it," I ordered. "Dad would be furious if he found out you were out here in pain or needed something and didn't call him."

"So would I," said Pastor Adams.

"Okay, okay." Cara laughed. Then her expression went serious again. "I don't know what I would have done without you guys today. Your father, Jacy. All of you. Emily was pretty scared and I wasn't sure what to do. I was guiding her. She wouldn't have been able to go for help on her own. A white cane alone just wouldn't be enough up here."

"The Lord takes care," Pastor Adams said.

"He sure does."

It seemed to me that Dad had taken care. And we had. Not some far-off God. If "the Lord" really was "taking care" of Cara Benoit, why hadn't He just manipulated circumstances to prevent her ankle from breaking in the first place?

It was a question for another day.

Or for never.

"Jacy, wake up!"

Dakota's whispering and shaking my shoulder gradually ousted my dream and I opened my eyes. "What?"

It was charcoal gray-blue in the tent. A combination of the dark of night, the moonlight, and the rainfly. What could Dakota possibly want at this hour?

"Something's wrong with Dad," he said. "Wake up."

"What do you mean something's wrong with Dad?" I sat up in my sleeping bag and attempted to fully wake myself by shaking my head.

"He just rushed out of here."

"Maybe Cara called for him?"

"No," Dakota said. "I've been wide awake. Nobody called Dad. Nobody called anyone."

"*You* were wide awake?" I laughed and then lay back down. "Dakota, he probably just had to—"

"He didn't zip the tent shut."

That was unusual. We always zipped the tent shut.

"I don't think he's feeling well," Dakota said. "He's been coughing a lot. I don't know how you've been able to sleep."

I pushed my sleeping bag back and got out of it. I felt around the foot of the tent until I found my boots and my flashlight. "We better go check on him."

"That's what I was thinking."

Neither Dakota nor I liked walking around outside the tent in the dark of night. Even with a flashlight, and even on a night when the moon was full, the closeness of the huge darkness intimidated me. Years of coming up here hadn't unsharpened my nervousness either. And since it was a fear that Dad allowed and sometimes even encouraged, I felt that it must be justified.

Locating Dad once Dakota and I had gotten outside the tent and tightly zipped the screen was not a problem. We wouldn't even have needed our flashlights, his coughing was so persistent. But we did use our lights and made our way down to the edge of the water.

I stood on one side of Dad and Dakota stood on the other. We clicked off our flashlights and our eyes quickly adjusted to the moonlight, its reflection on the water, and the light from the stars.

A person could actually see out here, I took a moment to notice. But only a moment. "Dad, what are you doing down here?" I asked him when he'd finally quit coughing.

He leaned forward with his hands on his knees and hung his head. "Couldn't breathe," he said. The effort started him coughing again.

"It's freezing out," I said.

"I didn't want to keep everyone awake."

"All right." After asking Dakota to bring our sleeping bags from the tent, I grabbed hold of Dad's arm and led him away from the water to a spot where we could sit down and have a boulder to lean against. He was hot. Shaking.

When Dakota brought the sleeping bags, we unzipped them all the way, spread one of them out on the ground and over part of the boulder, sat on it—Dakota and I on either side of Dad—and covered ourselves with the other two.

"I guess I was coming down with something after all," Dad said to me.

"I guess so," I said, recalling our conversation at "my" rock.

"I'm sorry," he said.

"Dad—"

"Listen to me, Jace," he said. "Dakota. I don't think I'm going to be able to hike this group out of here."

That much was abundantly obvious.

"You two will have to."

"What?" Dakota sat forward to turn toward Dad. "Really?" He sounded almost excited by the prospect.

I, however, was frightened by it. "Dad, we've never—"

"Pastor Adams will help you," he said. "I trust him."

"No, Dad," I said. "Nothing against Pastor Adams, but I'm not leaving you, or letting you leave me, or whatever it is you're thinking. No."

"I'm thinking," he said, "that I'll go out tomorrow with the guys when they come for Cara and Emily, and you two and Pastor Adams can hike everyone the rest of the way across."

"No," I said.

"We can do it, Jacy," Dakota insisted.

"We'll hike them back out the way we came," I said. "It's shorter."

"They didn't pay us to do that," Dad said. "They—" He leaned forward coughing again.

"They'll live," I said.

"Jace, this is business," Dad said. He barely had breath for the words.

When he leaned back against the boulder again, I pulled the sleeping bag to his chin and told him not to worry about it now. We would do the right thing. We would do what he thought we needed to do.

Just please don't try to talk anymore, Dad. You're scaring me.

Dad settled into a feverish half-sleep between Dakota and me. Even though neither of us slept, we didn't talk. We watched the moon inch its way across the sky. We took turns tending to Dad when he startled awake coughing. We navigated our separate emotions about what Dad had asked us to do.

Hike the rest of the trail.

Without him.

Something-teen miles.

The actual task of hiking the trail wasn't what was disconcerting to me. I'd hiked it tens of times before. We would survive. But being apart from Dad when he was sick? Wondering how he was and having no means of finding out?

I leaned against his shoulder and forced myself to think about the technicalities of hiking the trail. I'd have to talk with Dakota and Pastor Adams about Neil D'Ary. Someone would have to take on the position of decision maker as to how far we'd hike a day, where we'd set up camp, what time we'd leave in the morning, who would do what camp duties, when to indulge in rest stops. All that. And someone would have to decide whether we should put the group in the get-across-the-trail-as-quickly-as-possible mode or allow them the two-and-a-half remaining days that they'd paid for. I knew that I didn't want to be in charge. Dakota probably wouldn't want to either. But it wouldn't be fair to put it all on Pastor Adams. He was a customer, after all. I was sure Dad would expect Dakota or me to handle it.

Back Trails Unlimited was our business.

At the first sign of first light I left Dad and Dakota to make my way silently to Pastor Adams's tent. I wanted to talk with him before anyone else woke up. It took only two taps on his rainfly with my knuckles to rouse him. He asked me for a couple of minutes and then met me down at the water where Dakota and I had found Dad just hours before.

I summarized the situation for him and then watched while he walked over to talk with Dad. I waited anxiously for him to come back to the water's edge to tell me what he thought.

Maybe he'd be able to convince Dad that the hikers would rather turn back than hike further in without an adult guide . . . even though a guide was not required to hike the trail and Dakota and I certainly did know what we were doing. Maybe he'd be able to relieve Dad of his stubborn sense of obligation to see these hikers to the end of the trail. He could certainly offer them a refund or guarantee them a trip at reduced price—or at no cost—next summer. Maybe he'd be able to make Dad understand that I'd be worried sick about him. Wasn't his daughter more important than his business?

I licked my lips and shook my head.

That last thought wasn't fair and I knew it.

Dakota and I were more important to Dad than *Back Trails Unlimited* would ever be. It was simply that he didn't perceive this situation as an either-or. I wouldn't be able to do anything to help him most likely, even if I did go down the trail with him. I'd be just as worried at his side if he stayed as ill as he was currently or grew worse as I would be here on the trail, though I did think that knowing would make it a little easier.

One way or the other, these hikers had to walk somewhere. Nobody was going to fly up to Fossil Lake to pick them up. Someone from *Back Trails Unlimited* should go with them, and Dakota and I would both be much more confident and much better off if we worked at this together.

When Pastor Adams came and stood beside me again, he shoved his hands into his pockets and drew a circle in the dirt with the toe of his boot. "Are you okay with this, Jacy?"

"Not exactly," I confessed.

"But you'll do it for your dad."

It wasn't a question, but I nodded anyway. "I'd do just about anything for him, Pastor Adams." I felt tears at my eyes. They embarrassed me, so I swiped angrily at them.

"He definitely needs to be taken off this mountain and given medical attention," he said. Then he looked cautiously at me. "I think he's made the best decision about what happens after that."

"You do?"

"Yes."

"That helps, I guess," I said.

"Why don't you go get the fire going while I get all your dad's, Cara's, and Emily's gear together so the horses can haul it down with them instead of us having to figure out what to do with it."

"Okay."

"You know," he said, "if this had to happen, it couldn't have happened at a better time. I mean, we've already got people on the way up here to help Cara and Emily out. If your dad had to wait another day or half day, I'm not so sure we'd be able to keep him doing well."

"This didn't have to happen."

"People get sick, Jacy. It's the world we live in. And on top of that, your dad has had a rough couple of days that probably brought it on stronger than it might otherwise have come on."

That was true. Having to stay awake all night to make sure no more porcupines terrorized Sophie Sullivan. Getting caught in that rain and hail storm with Neil D'Ary and freezing all night on account of it. Hiking down to Kersey Lake and back in one day to find help for Cara Benoit and her niece.

"The timing was fortunate," I said. But then I glared at Pastor Adams. "I suppose you'd give your God the credit for that?"

He laughed. "I give God credit for being sovereign," he said. "I'm not completely sure I fully understand how that trickles down to all the little affairs of our everyday lives. I know He doesn't make us turn to Him. I know He doesn't make us do all the wrong things we do. I know He doesn't make us do the right things we do. But He is sovereign. I suppose that if He'd really wanted to get your dad's attention and make him completely miserable, He could have kept his body well today to wake up tomorrow morning sick. Seven, eight, or nine miles farther away from help and with nobody on their way up."

"But if He is sovereign," I argued, "He also could have kept Dad from getting sick in the first place."

"I believe He could have intervened and done that if that had been His will, yes."

"Why wouldn't it be His will for Dad to be well?"

"Have you ever baby-sat?" he asked me.

"What?"

"Have you ever baby-sat?"

I shook my head. "Although I feel like we are sometimes with some of the spoiled teenagers that come on our trips."

He laughed. "Okay. So you have in your mind when you set out how the trail should be hiked. You know how everyone should perform. You know what you should be able to feasibly accomplish on every given portion of the journey."

"Yeah." I had no idea where he was trying to go with this line of reasoning, but I decided to give him a chance to lead me around to it. Pastors were famous for doing that, I'd been told. Taking stories that seemed to have nothing to do with what they were talking about and using them to perfectly illustrate whatever point it was they were trying to make.

"But your hikers are not little robots. They don't always know what you expect, and many of them probably wouldn't care even if they did know."

That definitely described some of our experiences with some of our hikers.

"You still have to get them to the end of the trail," he said.

"We have to make adjustments," I said.

"Right. And it's kind of like that for God. He didn't program us to be little robots who automatically serve Him and get through the journey in the most efficient manner. Sometimes we trip. Sometimes we whine. Sometimes we ignore His leading. Sometimes we defy it outright. Sometimes we think we know a shortcut, or a better way, or even a better destination. Sometimes we blame Him for our sore feet when it was we who chose to wear pumps instead of hiking boots. But God is still going to get His creation to the end of the journey. The end of the Book."

"He has to make adjustments," I said.

"I don't know that I'd word it exactly like that, but He's working with a fallen people in a fallen world. Sometimes He has to do drastic things to get our attention, like making Balaam's donkey talk."

"And swallowing Jonah in the big fish." I waved his comments away. "Yeah, yeah, yeah. I heard you and Dad talking about that. Are you saying that Dad being sick is God's way of getting his attention? I don't really understand the connection."

"I know that God is trying to get your dad's attention." He shrugged. "He tries to draw all of us to Himself."

I laughed. "You didn't answer the question."

"That's because I can't answer that question. I couldn't say for sure that God caused this to happen any more than I could say for sure that He didn't. I can say for sure that He can use it to bring about His perfect will in your father's heart." He shooed a sluggish mosquito away from his face. "And in yours."

"Right now," I told him, "I'm not at all interested in the spiritual well-being of my heart. All I want to do is get safely through the next couple of days and back to Dad."

"I'm here to help you do that," he said.

The normal routines of morning seemed to drag along in slow motion until the two FWP guys arrived on horseback leading two other horses behind them. Then everything happened too quickly. I barely made it over to Dad to hand his jacket to him and say good-bye.

One of the FWP guys lifted Cara Benoit onto one of the horses and then helped Emily to climb on in front of her. Then he held Dad's arm while Dad struggled to hoist himself into the saddle of the second horse. "Hayden, if you need—"

"I'm fine," Dad snapped at him.

"Right," the FWP guy said as he grabbed the rope that was lying over the horse's back. The man's name was Todd. He'd been working this trail each summer for the past two years, so we knew him. "I'm going to lead your horse." He grinned, though he was obviously more concerned than amused, and tapped Dad's knee. "If you let me know *before* you fall off, Hayden, I might be able to grab your sleeve or something and save you a concussion on top of whatever it is you've got."

"I'll try to do that," Dad said. He'd taken the edge off his tone, but I could still see it in the frustrated tightness of his jaw. But even that softened instantly when he looked at Dakota and me. "Come here," he said to us.

We did.

"You guys be careful."

It hadn't occurred to me until then that in deciding to send us the rest of the way across the trail, Dad was setting himself up for as much worry as Dakota and me. Maybe more. He would get down the mountain and put himself in the hands of people who were trained to deal with his situation. People who would take care of him. Me and Dakota? We'd be up in the wilderness where anything could happen with the burden of twelve hikers relying on us to make all the right decisions.

Fortunately for all of us, Pastor Adams had agreed to step in and help and was competent to do so.

I squeezed Dad's hand tightly in mine. "We'll be careful. Don't worry, okay? Just get better."

"See you in a couple of days," he said.

Dakota and I stepped back from his horse, and Todd led him away from us back toward the trail.

"Jacy," Cara Benoit called to me as she gently directed her horse to make the same turn Dad's horse had just made, "I'll make sure he's taken care of until you guys get back."

I nodded and lifted my hand slowly to wave to her.

She waved back.

I said *thank you* but my voice had come in barely a whisper, and Cara had turned away already before I'd finished getting the words out. I didn't think she'd heard or seen.

Dakota stepped in next to me and put his arm over my shoulders. "When we turn around," he whispered, "we have to have it together, so don't turn around until you're ready."

I didn't think I'd ever be ready, but I swallowed hard and turned around as soon as Dad's horse topped the hill and began to make its way down the other side.

"Well," I said to Pastor Adams and the other eleven hikers who were all staring silently at Dakota and me, "let's pack up camp and move out. We've got lots of hiking to do today to make up for yesterday, and this part of the trail is the stuff of postcards."

I hurried past them and into my tent to change into one of my T-shirts with our logo on the front pocket. I had one each in red, green, teal, and yellow. I chose teal.

Maybe I'd feel more like an official trail guide if I looked like one.

CHAPTER **13**

We hiked.

Well above timberline. Through snow banks. Past a spot on the trail where there was an unobstructed view of the back of Granite Peak, the highest point in Montana at over twelve thousand feet. Down into timber again. To and past Dewey Lake where we stopped and ate the fish we caught—cutthroat trout, golden trout, and brookies—for lunch. We enjoyed a brief rest at Twin Outlets Lake, which is where we would have camped the previous night had we not been held over at Fossil Lake. All the hikers and Pastor Adams stopped to photograph waterfalls whenever we passed one. They photographed the surrounding mountains. They photographed a moose Dakota spotted along the creek bed, and a wolverine. They photographed one another.

As we walked along the seemingly never-ending switchbacks down to Duggan Lake, I felt as if I had shifted my mind into some kind of autopilot mode. I barely noticed the scenery except to point it out to the hikers. I didn't feel hungry . . . or thirsty . . . or tired, though I knew that I must be all of those since we were hiking so far and since I'd gotten almost no sleep the night before.

Whenever one of the hikers tried to talk with me, I hid behind facts about the trail or Pilot's and Index Peaks or the old mining days legend of Liver Eatin' Johnson or the history of Cooke City. To avoid having to walk with Pastor Adams, who'd be able to see right through all my prattling on, I positioned myself in front of Sophie Sullivan and behind Candice and their parents. I had clued Pastor Adams in to Dad's concerns about Neil D'Ary, and he'd taken it upon himself to safeguard that situation. Dakota was pulling the rear position in sight of the newlyweds and the two guys from Germany.

At my request, insistence, everyone was sticking a lot more closely to the "pack" than before. They were also being a lot more agreeable and protective over Dakota and me. None of them mentioned Dad, but I didn't doubt that they were thinking about him.

Praying for him.

I tried to pray for him. That he'd get off the mountain without falling off his horse or going unconscious from lack of oxygen during one of his fits of coughing. I tried to pray that he wouldn't dream about Mom because of his fever. I even tried to ask God to give Cara patience with Dad because he tended to be downright disagreeable and cranky about allowing others to help him.

But praying didn't come all that naturally to me and it seemed only to heighten my frustration with the whole God Question. Still, for Dad, I did it.

We crossed rough wooden bridges or logs or boulders or else hiked straight through the water of the creeks before Rainbow Lake. We stopped there and made camp for the night. Pastor Adams assigned the camp duties, put his tent up, and then supervised while the Sullivan girls put theirs up all on their own for the first time. Then he took Ezra, the newlyweds, and Mr. D'Ary down to the lake to help him catch some fish for dinner.

I recruited Neil D'Ary to help me collect firewood. "Unless your wrist is still bugging you," I said.

"It's not."

"Great."

I showed Neil what we were looking for: wood that wasn't still green. It needed to snap when you folded it in half, not bend.

"There are quite a few other people here," Neil observed after we'd worked for several minutes without speaking. "I even saw some horses."

"People come this far in from the other side all the time," I told him. "It's a good weekend trip."

"It's not a weekend."

"That's why it's only this busy." I smiled. "We never put ourselves here on a weekend. Not when we've got a group with us and will need a site big enough for five or six tents." I bent to grab a completely dried-up branch from the ground underneath one of the huge old trees that surrounded the lake on all sides. "We come up here on our own sometimes on our off weekends."

"I'd think you guys would go to the city for your off weekends," he said.

"Nah." I smiled. "We only do that when we need to do our shopping."

When neither of us could possibly carry another piece of wood, we started heading back toward camp. The pine needles that covered the ground in layers in this thick and ancient section of forest crunched beneath our boots as we walked. Nothing grew on the ground because of the needles and because the sunlight was held at the tops of the branches by the thickness of the moss covered trees and their closeness to one another. It was a cool and peaceful place, although it did possess a certain eeriness.

"Everyone should come up here," Neil said after a while. "At least once."

"You're enjoying it then?"

"Yeah," he answered right away. "It kind of tweaks at your perspective."

"What do you mean?" I asked, even though I thought I already knew. People had often commented to us that their trip had helped them pull back from their normal stresses enough to make them wonder if they hadn't perhaps swerved from their focus somewhere along the line.

My relationship with my daughter is more important than the fact that she married that loser I told her not to marry.

My time is more important to my children than my ability to buy them every little thing their hearts could desire.

Yeah, my parents think that their way of doing things is the only way to do things and they annoy me to tears every time we visit, but my children need to know their grandparents.

My wife could die tomorrow and I haven't said the words "I love you" since our first anniversary in 1981.

Things like that.

"I came on this trip to get a break from my dad," Neil said. "I made all the arrangements without telling him. I drove away without saying good-bye. I didn't want him even to know where I was." He stepped over a fallen log and lost one of his pieces of wood.

"Leave it," I told him. "If you try to pick it up, you'll be picking it all up."

He nodded. "But he found out where I was and he showed up here and your dad made room for him to come along—"

My shoulders tensed. "My dad *had* room, Neil. He didn't make room."

"That came out wrong," he said.

I suspected that it had come out in complete accordance with Neil's feelings about it, though he might not have intended to voice them.

"I'm sorry," he said.

I forced myself to breathe out slowly and forbade myself to embrace Neil's statement as a personal attack against my father. I acknowledged to myself that I just might be feeling overly defensive of Dad because of the current situation and my distress about it.

But I did not acknowledge anything aloud to Neil. "Okay. Go on."

"I think I'm going to go home thinking that I've got to find a way to make things right between us," he said quietly. "I mean, he could . . . if something . . ." He sighed loudly, shook his head, and stopped walking to stare up through the tall trees. "If it would have been me in your situation this morning, putting my father on a horse and sending him away down the mountain realizing that he's sick enough that I might not get back in time to—" He snapped his mouth shut and looked at me. "I'm sorry. Jacy, I—"

"It's all right," I told him even though my hands had suddenly turned icy cold. "Dad's going to be fine. He's—"

"I'm sure he is."

"I . . . I think I know what you were working at saying," I said because I knew it was a good thing for Neil to be thinking along these lines and because I had to brake and backtrack my own thinking before it sped out of control in the wrong direction.

It wasn't as if the possibility Neil had been about to mention hadn't already occurred to me a thousand times over.

Ignore it, I told myself. What else could I do?

"All there would be is regret," Neil said finally. "I don't want it like that."

We began walking again.

"Have you talked to your dad, Neil? About this?"

"A little," he said. "I was only brave enough because Pastor Adams was with us. I figured, you know, he's a pastor. He's supposed to know how to deal with junk like this."

"And did he?"

Poor Pastor Adams. Some vacation this was turning out to be.

"He said some stuff that made a lot of sense," Neil said. "Yeah."

"That's good. How'd your dad seem to take it?"

Neil dropped his stack of wood next to the spot where Dakota had put together rocks to form a ring for the fire. Then he stepped aside so I could drop mine. "I don't know. He just stayed quiet."

I smiled as I rubbed my hands together to get the dirt and chips of bark off them. "That's how my dad is all the time."

"It's kind of scary," he said.

"Yeah," I agreed quietly, "it kind of is."

I supposed that in Neil's case his father's silence, though frightening to Neil because it was unfamiliar, probably represented progress. It could mean that he was thinking through what his son had said instead of just venting the first emotion that came to mind.

My father's silences, though, rarely represented progress. They were just his way of keeping his calm. Keeping even. Keeping control.

On the outside.

On the inside? He was keeping pain.

Somehow, though I'd been watching Dad avoid his feelings about Mom's death for as long as I could remember, I had not seen it as a "scary" thing until this trip. It was just the way it was. And even if it didn't always feel completely right, it still felt a whole lot safer than being around someone who fell apart every other day.

But Pastor Adams—his God?—had seen what I hadn't been able or willing or brave enough or old enough to see. My father, who I'd always thought of as the strongest person in the world, did need. Not more than the next guy, maybe, but certainly enough that *I* would never be able to remedy it.

"So . . ." Neil rubbed his hands together in front of him and then pointed down at the empty fire pit. "Do you think you could teach me how to get one of these things started?"

I smiled. *That* I could do.

With Neil and his father being noncombative for the first time during the trip, and Sophie and Candice being nonannoying, our time around the campfire that evening was actually pleasant. The way it usually was. The way it was supposed to be. We talked. We joked. We sang a couple of songs—not German.

Sophie almost fell backwards off the boulder she was sitting on when Neil D'Ary sat beside her and told her she looked great in her pale yellow sweatshirt (even though it had gotten a bit dirty) and asked her if she had a boyfriend. She did manage to answer him that yes, she did have a boyfriend, but she was sure they'd break up eventually . . . maybe even as soon as she returned home.

"Oh brother," Dakota whispered to me.

I laughed, and then nodded appreciatively at Pastor Adams. I had no idea what he'd said to Neil D'Ary, but clearly, it had helped.

His expression remained watchful.

"How about you, Jacy?" Neil asked. "Do you have a boyfriend?"

I didn't miss Sophie's sulky response or Dakota's disgusted one or Pastor Adams's warning glance. I laughed. I couldn't help it. "Neil, I think my dad would choke on his coffee if I even mentioned the possibility."

"Yeah," Dakota said, laughing too. "Dad can handle bears and lightning and broken bones and stuff, but some teenaged boy with actual feelings for *Jacy*?"

"Like it would be so impossible." I smacked my brother.

"I don't think it would be impossible at all," Neil said.

"Ooooo," sang the Sullivan girls in unison.

I looked at Pastor Adams. "Do something."

He smiled and held up his hands.

"Anyone would choke on your dad's coffee, Jacy," Neil said. Then, more seriously, he added, "You should talk to him about it."

"Neil," I said, "realistically, there are no guys my age or even close that live anywhere near me. All the guys I meet are only around for five or six days, or maybe the whole summer if there's someone working in Cooke City that I might think I might like. But they're generally college guys who are way too old for me, and we're gone all the time anyway, so . . ." I shrugged. "It's just not an issue right now."

"Hey," Mr. Sullivan said, nudging his wife, "maybe we should think about moving up here."

"Ha, ha, ha." Candice stared sideways at her father. "Very funny."

"See, Dakota," I said. "All dads are weird about their daughters dating."

"There are no guys at your school?" Sophie asked me.

"Dad home schools us," Dakota told her.

"Really?"

"He teaches us," I clarified. "We aren't always at home."

"And this is . . . adequate?" one of the men from Germany wanted to know.

This led into an hour-long conversation about home schooling. Its virtues and its perceived shortcomings. Its appropriateness or lack thereof. The proof of its worth being evident in its statistical results. Its unique challenges. That was all fine with me. In fact, it was interesting to hear other peoples' perspectives. Especially those of the men from Germany and Pastor Adams. But then Quentin D'Ary started playing the analyst and dragging the conversation in the direction of my father. What did it say about him, his willingness to move us to the middle of nowhere to homeschool us and keep us so separated from the "real" world?

I told him flat-out and rudely that it was none of his business.

As if *he* was the perfect father and had done nothing but right by Neil.

Please.

"What it says to me," Pastor Adams said quietly when I'd finished, "is that Hayden Craig took a situation in his life that drives lots of lesser men to do lots of lesser things and made the decisions for his remaining family that made the most sense and seemed the most workable to him. Jacy and Dakota are as well adjusted, intelligent, and happy as any other kids—more than a lot of kids—only maybe they're a little bit less hardened, which just might be a good thing when you take a good honest look at what you call the 'real' world."

"You're right," Mr. D'Ary said simply. "You're absolutely right. I was wrong. I'm sorry."

As conversation slowly resumed about the probable age of the trees around us, I stared over the top of the fire at Pastor Adams.

What was it about him? He wasn't forceful or particularly charismatic. He didn't have a whole list of credentials and letters at the back of his name. He really didn't even say that much. And yet he'd gotten my father to read the whole Bible. He'd gotten me to think more about God during the past four days than I had in my entire life previously. And he'd just gotten Quentin D'Ary to shut up and admit out loud that he'd been wrong.

Impressive.

Not only did I not know what it was about him that made him so uncommonly compelling, I realized, I didn't know *anything* about him other than that he had a seventeen-year-old son named Ezra.

"You know," I said to him after a while, after everyone but he and Ezra and Dakota and me had gone to their tents, "I don't even know where you're from."

"Billings."

"You pastor a church there?"

"Yes."

"By yourself?"

"With an assistant pastor," he said.

"How long have you been doing that?"

"Nine years."

"At the same church?"

"Yes."

That surprised me, though I wasn't sure why. Maybe it was because of another pastor we'd had on one of our trips recently. He'd just been voted out, and it was his assertion that some churches went through pastors like most people went through bottles of shampoo. Use them up, throw them out, try a new brand. Apparently, Pastor Adams's church had found the "brand" that worked for them. "I take it you do a lot of this outdoor stuff?"

"As much as I can sneak in," he said, smiling.

"Can I ask you something?"

He laughed. "You mean you haven't been?"

"I was just amassing information," I said. "The question I want to ask now is deeper than that."

"I'll do my best to answer it," he promised. "Shoot."

I glanced down at the toe of my boot and then pushed at one of the fire ring stones with it. "How did you get my father to talk to you? I mean, about more than your rafting trip?"

"I talked to him," he said.

"Other people have tried that and have only offended him."

"Maybe because they haven't been there," he said. "Your father caught me right in the middle of being there."

I didn't understand.

"In all your questions," he said, "you didn't ask me about my wife."

"I guess I just figured she's not into the camping thing," I said.

"She wasn't," he said.

Wasn't.

Then I understood. "When did she . . ."

"Early last spring."

"It was a skiing accident," Ezra explained.

"I'm sorry." The words were stupid and useless. I knew that. Inadequate.

Ezra stood and moved closer to the fire. Closer to his father. "It was one of those freak things that ninety-nine times out of a hundred wouldn't have happened," he said.

I nodded. My mother had died from a flu virus. Something that ninety-nine times out of a hundred a person would get and get over.

"Kind of like Mom," Dakota said.

"Yes." Pastor Adams nodded. "Kind of like your mother." He reached to grab a stick from the woodpile and then started rearranging the burning logs in the fire with it. "The second night of that rafting trip last summer," he said without looking up from the end of his stick in the coals, "a bunch of us were sitting around the fire like this, and a couple of the guys got going on complaining about their wives. It got to me so I left and went down to the bank of the river where we'd pulled in our rafts." He looked up at Dakota and me. "Your father followed me. He said something like someday their wives are going to be gone and they're going to remember this night and all their laughing and they're going to hate themselves for it. I agreed, of course, and tried to laugh it off, but . . ."

"But Dad saw right through you," Dakota said, "because that's what he does."

"Right," Pastor Adams said. "I told him about my wife. He told me about your mother. We stood there for a good hour, silent, mostly. But then your father asked me if I had kids. I told him yes, I had Ezra. He told me I'd have to find a way to fight through it, a reason to fight through it, for Ezra. That's what he'd done."

The wind shifted then and smoke from the fire started blowing toward me, burning my eyes. But I didn't stand to move. For anyone who noticed them, it would account for my tears.

As if I'd need to account for them.

"I told your father I didn't see it like that," Pastor Adams continued. "That, yes, Ezra would need me to be strong for him, but no, that wasn't my only reason for going on. I had trusted God to be the author and finisher of my faith when my wife was alive and I thought I could see where He was taking me, and I still trusted Him. Somehow, He was going to lead me through this. This hadn't happened outside of His knowledge or love, and He was going to walk me through it for His glory." He shrugged, and then he smiled a little. "I don't suppose I have to tell you how your dad responded to that."

"I know how I would've responded," Dakota said. "For His glory? What are you, nuts?"

"Dakota!" I couldn't believe my brother had just said that.

But Pastor Adams was laughing. "That's exactly what your father said."

"Really?" Dakota visibly enjoyed the knowledge for a moment, but then his expression hardened again. "You'd think that for His glory, God could have done something good like make sure your wife didn't die so that He wouldn't have to help you through something so awful."

"That's pretty much what your dad said too," Pastor Adams said quietly.

"Well?"

"Dakota," I warned again in a whisper. Since when had my brother become so confrontational? He'd grown up to be a lot like Dad in that he didn't enter easily into conversations, and he certainly didn't probe for information so thoroughly embedded in the core of a man as his real-life faith. Aside from the obvious fact that it would be none of his business, he wouldn't want to dig there for fear of stirring things up and inspiring the person to probe back.

"It's all right, Jacy," Pastor Adams assured me. Then he looked back at Dakota. "I simply believe that as long as I'm His, God is going to take my life to the end that He has in mind for it, just like a writer gets his characters and his story to the end that he has in mind for them. There's a passage in the book of Hebrews that says, *Wherefore seeing we also are compassed about with so great a cloud of witnesses, let us lay aside every weight, and the sin which doth so easily beset us, and let us run with patience the race that is set before us, looking unto Jesus the author and finisher of our faith; who for the joy that was set before him endured the cross, despising the shame, and is set down at the right hand of the throne of God. For consider him that endured such contradiction of sinners against himself, lest ye be wearied and faint in your minds.*"

Pastor Adams paused for a couple of moments, I supposed to give Dakota and me time to try to make sense of what he'd just quoted. Then he said, "I'm sure all that sounds a little foreign to you, but I have found incredible confidence in those verses for just about my whole life, and now is no exception. God wants to teach me things. He wants me to grow to depend more and more fully on Him, and to understand and know Him more and more completely. He has things for me to accomplish. When things happen, He uses them to get me there. And He, Himself, has been through the worst of things. So, Dakota, the way I see it, my only real hope of getting through my wife's death with any kind of success and peace is saying, 'Okay, Lord, I don't know why You allowed this to happen, but I do know that *You* know and I trust You. So start the next chapter.' "

"Did you say all that to my dad?" I asked.

"Probably not as concisely," he said. "I've had a whole year since then to better put words to my thoughts. But basically, yes."

"What did he say?" Dakota wanted to know.

"Nothing."

I suspected that Dakota and I had just gotten the answer to our questions about Dad's esteem for Pastor Adams. Here was a man who, when Dad had first met him, had lost his wife within only months and yet seemed to know how he'd make peace with it. Dad was no fool. He would have recognized, as I did now, that spouting religious sounding assurances when things were rolling merrily along was one thing, but standing on them—even if with a little bit of clinging—when one's whole world had just been sucked out from underneath him . . . that was something else. Something to be respected. Something that meant something.

Something real.

CHAPTER **15**

I woke up because I'd heard a noise. By the time I'd fully dragged myself out of my dream though, I couldn't hear it anymore, and I couldn't remember what it was, exactly, that I had heard.

But I had definitely heard something.

So I lay there in the dark tent and waited to see whether or not I'd hear it again.

"Dakota?" I whispered after a while. "Dakota. Wake up."

"What?" he muttered.

"Shh," I warned.

He pulled his sleeping bag over his head and rolled onto his side facing away from me. "Go back to sleep," he said, and then did exactly that.

Wonderful.

Dad would have awakened instantly at my call. In fact he would have awakened before I had. He probably would have already figured out what had made the noise, and probably would have already done something about it.

But Dad wasn't there.

And Dakota was asleep. Useless.

Slowly I unzipped my sleeping bag enough to free my left arm and then reached along the side at the bottom of the tent for the mesh pouch where I'd placed Dad's handgun. Once it was in my hand, cold and heavy, I lay still again.

Silence, except for the wind among the trees.

My hand loosened its hold on Dad's handgun and I began the mental task of convincing myself that I hadn't really heard anything when I knew good and well that I had.

Maybe someone had walked by our tent on their way back from a midnight "restroom" run.

No. I would have heard a tent zipper.

Maybe a horse in one of the other camps had startled.

Maybe a moose had passed through on its way down to the water.

Maybe coyotes had disturbed our wood pile.

Maybe there was a crazed man-hating twelve-thousand-pound nothing but teeth and claws griz getting set to pounce on one of our hikers' tents. Or on my tent.

I shut my eyes and forced myself to breathe in slowly.

I would smell a bear.

A moose would pass right by us without incident as long as nobody spooked it and as long as it wasn't a mama with a calf.

Coyotes were nothing more than a harmless and noisy nuisance. *Be reasonable.*

There's nothing to be afraid of.

So why was I shaking?

"Because Dad's not here," I whispered to myself and then tensed at the sound of my own breathy voice in all the dark silence. Then I had to grin. "This is stupid."

I rolled onto my side, returned the handgun to the mesh pouch, rezipped my sleeping bag, and pulled it over my face. Whatever had made the noise I'd heard was probably long gone, and I'd most likely never find out what it had been since it wasn't raining and the ground was packed and dry. Maybe I'd find some tracks down by the water in the morning.

But then again, maybe I wouldn't even look.

Though fear eventually released its hold on me, wakefulness would not. The hardness of the ground beneath me as I lay there began to annoy me, and Dakota's relaxed and steady breathing began to sound so loud to me that I was blaming *it* for keeping me up. I refrained from nudging him only because I knew that the increased volume of his breathing was a flawed perception of mine and not reality. A person couldn't possibly breathe as loudly as my brother seemed to be breathing during those frustrating hours.

Thinking so much about breathing started me wondering how and where Dad might be, which only served to bully sleep even farther out of my reach. I wondered if they had put him in the hospital or if he'd been allowed to go home. I wondered if his fever had let up at all. I wondered if they'd given him something to help him breathe freely enough that he, at least, would be able to sleep through this horrible night. Knowing my father as well as I did, I also had to wonder if he hadn't just assured everyone that he was fine and gone home without even seeing a doctor.

No. Dad had looked to be in just about as much trouble as a sheep on its back when he'd left that morning. His "I'm fine" thing wouldn't convince a marmot let alone people with brains who knew him. Besides, Cara Benoit had promised me that she'd see to it that he was taken care of until we made it back. I believed her. Not because Dad had helped her, though Cara was clearly not one to forget something like that or underestimate its value, but because she had given me her word. Cara seemed like a person who would keep her word. It was that simple. She also seemed like a challenge chaser. Unafraid to tackle anything. A quality she'd definitely need to tap into if my father decided he'd rather not be looked after.

I squeezed my eyes shut and forced myself to think about nothing but sleeping.

Eventually dawn colored our tent teal.

I got up and busied myself with building the fire and starting a pot of water to boil.

Aside from the fact that it was usually cold, early morning was my favorite time of day in the mountains. Mosquitoes couldn't fly in the clingy cool dampness. Everything looked clearer, more defined, because of the severe angle of the sun. Colors seemed more intense. And even though the pervading odor was usually that of damp dirt and pine, everything smelled clean and new.

It was peaceful. Serene.

Until people started waking up. Spraying on foul smelling insect repellent. Stirring water into instant coffee or hot chocolate or spiced cider which all had potent aromas of their own. Zipping and unzipping tent and pack and jacket zippers. Whistling. Laughing. Walking around, usually in loosely tied boots, *thud thud thud* on the hard earth. Talking. Eating. Packing up camp.

Then the serenity took a back seat to the business of the trail . . . though it never quite left altogether. A person could invite it forward again at any moment in these mountains and it would come.

Usually.

"You're worried about your dad."

We'd hiked about a mile out of Rainbow Lake when Ezra stepped in behind me on the trail.

I laughed. "Is it that obvious? Even from behind?"

"It's pretty obvious," he said.

"Wouldn't you be?"

"Yeah, I would," he answered right away.

I laughed again. I couldn't help it. "Ezra, you're not supposed to say that. You're supposed to attempt to console me with some of that 'God is in control' nonsense of yours."

Ezra didn't laugh. "I don't use that expression."

I thought about apologizing. But only for a moment. "Why not?" I asked instead. "Don't you believe He is?"

"I believe He's sovereign."

"Oh, Ezra," I said, sighing, "what's the difference?" I was not in the mood for this kind of conversation.

"If you lie, is it God that makes you do it?" he asked me.

"Of course not."

"Then He doesn't control you. You have free will, which was His to grant you or not grant you."

"Because He's sovereign," I concluded.

"Right."

I supposed that if I took the time to dissect the concept as Ezra obviously had at some point in his own search to better understand the God he'd been raised to believe in, I'd likely concede the distinction. But I had no intention of taking the time. "I've never seen Dad that sick, is all."

"I think people like you and me tend to worry over our fathers more than most kids do," he said.

"Do you?"

"Yeah. They're all we've got, for one thing, aside from God."

That was true . . . at least up to the "aside from God" part.

"Plus," he said, "most kids just think of their fathers as *Dad*. The guy who grounds them. The guy whose car they want to borrow. The guy who got them that computer for their birthday. And hopefully the guy they could count on to be there for them no matter what. But me and you, we've seen our dads be human totally apart from us. Their own person, not just our *Dad*. Vulnerable. Someone who might need someone to be there for them."

True again.

"There is something I can say to console you," Ezra said seriously, "though I don't know if it will or not."

I smiled even though he wouldn't be able to see because he was behind me and my sleeping bag on top of my pack was higher than the top of my head. "What's that?"

"I'm praying for him. So's my dad."

"Truthfully," I said, "I'm beginning to get the impression that if there is a God, your dad is one person who has definitely established a connection with Him. So that does help. Thanks."

We walked until late morning and then stopped to fish one of the streams. This day's hike would not be particularly strenuous, so we could afford to take breaks lengthy enough to actually enjoy.

And I did enjoy them.

First of all because the day itself was perfect. Cool. Sunny. Not at all humid.

The scenery, as always, was gorgeous.

Our hikers overall were content. They seemed to be appreciating the trip now and were no longer caring that they were dirty. They'd become more realistic and relaxed about the possibility of a bear encounter, had adjusted to the lack of fine cuisine, and had settled in to the unique demands and routines of life on a trail.

Mostly, though, I enjoyed the breaks because of the attention I was receiving from Neil D'Ary and Ezra Adams. Both of them seemed to want to be around me.

It was an unexpected and surprisingly engaging distraction from so much anxiety about Dad.

"I'll walk with you, Jacy."

"Let me help you with your pack, Jacy."

"You must be in great shape, Jacy, doing this all the time."

"That color suits you, Jacy."

I wasn't about to let their attention go to my head. They both knew that I'd rather be with Dad than hiking this trail and were probably just trying to make it easier for me.

But I wasn't planning to complain either.

Even with all the breaks we'd taken, we had camp set up at Elk Lake by four o'clock that afternoon. This left us plenty of time to fish, swing in Dad's portable hammock, nap, and collect enough wood to insure a fire that would last well into the night in honor of it being our last night on the trail.

"It's almost depressing," Sophie Sullivan said to me as the two of us sat on a boulder on the shore of the lake skimming the surface of the water with our bare feet. "I'm just getting used to it up here and tomorrow we'll be going home."

I nodded and smiled. It was a common enough sentiment. "You could always come again next year. We do have a lot of repeat customers . . . until they've been up here enough to realize that they could do this trail on their own. We see them sometimes."

"I think one of the guys from Germany has talked my father into taking us to see him and his family next summer," she said.

"Well," I said, "that would be fun too."

"I don't want to go to Germany," she said.

I leaned toward her until our shoulders were nearly touching. "If I remember that first day at all, Sophie, it would be my guess that you hadn't wanted to come *here* either."

Her quick smile revealed her embarrassment at the recollection. "I can't believe I asked your father to carry my plate." She laughed. "What an idiot. And I can't believe I screamed my head off over a porcupine."

"The porcupine thing was understandable," I assured her.

She laughed again. "But not the plate thing?"

"I have to admit, that was a new one," I said.

"Your dad probably thinks I'm the world's biggest loser."

I lowered my feet into the water to my ankles and stiffened for a second at the cold. "He doesn't think that way, Sophie." I pressed my chin to my chest and deepened my voice to quote Dad. "It's not our job or place to think anything. We get them over the trail. That's it. That's what we think about. That's what we do. That's where it ends." I pulled my feet out of the water before the experience went from refreshing to numbing. "Besides," I told Sophie, "we had the world's biggest loser on one of our hikes already. Two summers ago. He was always goofing off. Dancing on the edges of cliffs, pretending to be stumbling out of control toward the fire, yelling 'bear' all the time. He pretended to lose his footing once on one of those stretches of the trail on the rockslides that go down to the lakes."

Sophie nodded. I had her full attention. If there was any element of the trail that could be construed as precarious in and of itself and scary, it was those stretches. To the hikers' left, the mountain rose up steeply in the broken, crumbly, slippery, loose rock of ancient rockslides. To the right, the mountain continued down the same way, ending up in a lake at the bottom, sometimes several hundred feet below the trail, which was barely wide enough in spots to walk on. Slick dirt and rocks.

I looked steadily at Sophie. "Dad turned around to grab him when he yelled out, and *he* really slipped."

"Oh, no," Sophie said.

"Yeah," I said. "With his pack on and on that loose ground with nothing to grab onto, he slid all the way down the slope and into the lake. He could have drowned. He could have broken his neck. Some of those lakes are so deep that we might never have recovered his body if he had drowned. And the guy just kept saying, 'It was a joke, man,' over and over again as if that made it okay." I shuddered and shook my head, surprised by the potency of my anger at the memory of those seemingly endless seconds when the water grew still after Dad had fallen through it before he'd been able to get loose of his pack and swim back up to the surface. "Sophie, nothing you did or could even have imagined doing would come close to that guy in the loser department, so don't worry about it, okay? My father doesn't think you're a loser."

"Okay," she said. "Was he okay? Your dad?"

"He was banged up, cold, had scraped nearly all the skin off both of his hands, and lost his pack and everything in it . . . but yeah, he was okay."

We laughed.

"He finished the trail with us," I said. "This is the first time Dakota and I have ever had to hike it without him."

"I'd never have guessed that," she said. "You guys have taken over like you do this all the time."

"You think so? Thanks." But, really, what else could we have done? Sit on a boulder in a stubborn shivering heap and refuse to move? Right. "It's helped to have Pastor Adams along," I confessed.

Sophie smiled, but it was evident in the rest of her expression, and especially in the way she diverted her eyes from mine, that she was not fond of the pastor.

"I know," I said. "But it's his job to be preachy. That's what he's supposed to do."

"He's supposed to be on vacation," she said.

I shrugged. "I guess when you really believe something, you never go on vacation from it."

"Well, the rest of us are on vacation. If we wanted to hear preaching, we'd have gone on a drive-through tour of the Bible Belt with the radio on."

I laughed. "A lot of what he says does make sense. Don't you think so?"

"Ah," she said and dismissed the question with an impatient wave of her hand, "I never listen to him. As soon as he opens his mouth I tune him out because I know it's going to be preaching. Like that first day at dinner when he told us we shouldn't idolize Neil because he might be as needy on the inside as the next guy." She shook her head and tossed a rock into the water. "Give me a break."

Apparently Sophie had been "tuning out" Neil D'Ary as well if she hadn't figured out by now that he indeed *was* needy on the inside.

"I mean, Neil is great-looking." Sophie giggled. "I love his green eyes. And he's rich. He's got the best life, traveling all around to all the world's great places like London and Melbourne and Paris." She leaned back with her hands on the boulder behind her and stared up through the branches above her at the deep blue sky.

The dreamy look on her face turned my stomach. "Sophie," I said, "those are all outside things. None of them matter or can consistently make everything good if you're hurting and confused on the inside." I thought of Pastor Adams. And of Ezra. "Just like if you're really at peace on the inside, nothing that happens on the outside has to topple you."

Sophie Sullivan stared at me as if I'd just spoken to her in Flemish. "Whatever, Jacy." She grabbed her socks and boots, stood up, mumbled something about needing to find a warmer shirt, and left me alone at the edge of the water.

Realizing that *I* had just "preached" someone right out of my presence, I couldn't help chuckling a little. It was, to say the least, previously unvisited ground for me. Sermonizing at a customer. But I hadn't intended it to be that. I'd simply stated something that had suddenly clicked into perfectly clear focus for me. I wondered if that's what it was like for people who understood all the God-stuff. Getting repeatedly rejected, misunderstood, and accused of philosophizing, moralizing, pontificating, looking down their "holier-than-thou" noses, preaching, judging . . . when in actuality all they were doing was telling it how they saw it and wondering how on earth the person they were talking to could fail to see it too.

It had to be terribly frustrating.

I heard someone behind me and turned to see Neil D'Ary spinning away from and swatting at a bee. Only when he was sure it intended to leave him alone did he start walking toward me again.

"Do you mind if I sit here with you?" he asked me.

I smiled up at him. He did have exceptional green eyes, I took the time to observe. "Why would I mind?"

He sat carefully on the boulder beside me, obviously wanting to avoid getting wet. "Sometimes people want to be alone is all."

"Nah," I said. "There're more bees here than up higher."

"I noticed."

"Are you okay?"

"I'm only not okay if one stings me." He sounded tense and self-conscious. Like he'd rather be talking about some tournament semifinal that he'd lost in three sets.

"Do you like snowmobiling?" I asked him.

He laughed. "That was random."

"I was just trying to change the subject."

"Oh," he said. "Thanks. I've never been snowmobiling."

"You should come back here this winter. We could take—"

"I'll be back to tennis by then."

"That's right." I grinned. "While I'm outside in thigh-deep snow with my teeth chattering helping Dad move and stack more firewood, you'll be soaking up the sun down under right in the middle of their summer."

"It is kind of nice," he said.

"You'll have to send me a T-shirt."

"I will," he promised. "Unless you think it'll get your dad choking on that coffee of his."

"He does make better coffee at the house." The sun had dried my feet enough that I thought I'd be able to get my socks back on, so I leaned back to pull them from the branch where I'd hung them. "Just send a T-shirt for him and Dakota too. Then he won't think anything of it."

"I'll do it."

"Great."

Then we went silent. It wasn't comfortable silence exactly, but it wasn't uncomfortable, either. I finished getting my socks and boots back on and then just watched the water gently tapping up against the boulder we were sitting on. Neil appeared to be doing the same thing, and it did appear to be having the same soothing affect on him that it always had on me.

But then Mr. D'Ary came and stood behind us.

For several minutes, that's all he did. Stood there. Hovering almost. But eventually, quietly, he said, "Lots of bees around."

Neil stiffened. "Yes, sir."

Half expecting Mr. D'Ary to order Neil into his tent, I moved to get to my feet.

"I remember the first time you had a reaction to getting stung," Mr. D'Ary said. "Have you ever seen that happen, Jacy?"

"No."

"It was terrifying. I was sure Neil was going to die. No matter what I did, it didn't help. He couldn't breathe. He couldn't talk to me. He kept grabbing at me with this look in his eyes like *Why can't you fix this, Dad? Please fix this!* and—"

"I . . . that's not what I was thinking."

"I vowed," Mr. D'Ary said, "when it was all over and we were at the hospital and they told me that you were going to be okay, that I would never allow you into a situation again where I wouldn't be able to fix it if something went wrong because—"

"You never told me that." Neil looked up from the water and then turned to face his father. He looked shaken.

So did Mr. D'Ary when I stood up and offered him my spot on the boulder, which he silently accepted.

They stayed there until evening when Pastor Adams announced that the fish were done for anyone who was hungry. When they joined the rest of the group at the fire, they ate side by side. They were quiet as we sat around and talked afterwards, but not tense. And when they left the fire to turn in for the night, they both went to the same tent.

I glanced over at Pastor Adams after they'd gone, and caught him looking after them too. When he turned back to the fire and saw me looking at him, he said, "God is good, Jacy. You really can't count on anything else, but you can always count on that."

As we approached the bottom of the trail and East Rosebud the next noon, I kept the pace as quick as would be safe and kept looking ahead to see if I'd see Dad coming up to meet us. The steep and steady downhill of this part of the trail, though not strenuous in the same way as the uphill at the higher elevations, did take its toll on a hiker's knees and feet. It seemed like a constant effort to brake oneself from being lured into a full-out run down the mountain by gravity, the grade of the trail, and the weight of the packs. A full-out run might not be a bad thing on flat, level, clear ground, but this ground contained rocks and tree roots and washouts and piles of horse waste that one would prefer to avoid. All of it made difficult to see by the ever fluctuating shade and sunlight. A misstep could twist an ankle, propel someone face first into a tree, or hurl someone into the white, loud, rock-strewn water of the creek that the trail was following.

I slowed up a little.

Dad would not take kindly to having Candice Sullivan lose three of her teeth because of my hurry to see him. Besides, Dakota, Pastor Adams, and I had kept everyone safe up till now and it would be a slap in the face to have someone get injured an eighth of a mile from the end of the trail.

I led the group down into the valley, along one side of East Rosebud Lake, which was cluttered with cabins and summer homes, and onto the flat ground of the parking area at the trailhead.

Our big hunter green van was parked there with the trailer for the packs hitched to it, right where Dad always left it. He would hire one of the college kids working in Cooke City to drive a separate outfit down the day before we were to leave for a hike while he drove ours. Then he'd leave the van at the lake so that nobody would have to come meet us and ride back up as far as Cooke Pass with the guy or girl he'd hired. I knew that he had given his keys to Pastor Adams before going out with the FWP guys, so I wasn't worried about how we'd get home.

But I'd been counting on Dad being down here to meet us.

The fact that he wasn't could only mean that he was still too sick to come.

He'd know what time we'd likely hike out and he'd have come if he'd been able.

I tried to keep my disappointment and concern from showing in my face as I directed the hikers to get free of their packs and toss them into the trailer, but I knew that I was woefully failing. When I felt hands on my shoulders and heard Ezra quietly tell me to not be afraid, it was all I could do to not start crying . . . but I managed it.

The three-hour drive along the base of the mountains to Red Lodge and then back up the Beartooth Highway to Cooke Pass dragged by in what seemed like twice its normal time. I didn't even notice the breathtaking scenery on the Pass even though my eyes were directed right at it and even though the hikers behind me in the van couldn't quit commenting about it.

Dakota made mention of all the significant sights when we passed them—the spot on the switchbacks where you could look back up and see a wrecked car in the trees and rocks, the waterfall, Glacier Lake down in a rocky valley, the ski lift where the U.S. Olympic team sometimes practiced in the summer, West Summit, Pilot and Index Peaks, the turnoff to the Chief Joseph Scenic Highway, the road into Island Lake where we'd often see moose, the Top of the World Store, the start of the Morrison Jeep Trail.

I'd have to remember to thank Dakota.

Dad always pointed out the sights.

It hadn't even occurred to me to do so, and I was certain I would have missed half of them even if it had.

When we finally arrived at the house, Dakota and I obeyed Pastor Adams when he told us to go straight to Dad's office to check our messages.

"Ezra and I will get the packs out," he said.

There were several messages from people who wanted to book or cancel spots on one of Dad's fall hunting trips. There was a message from Grandma Craig thanking Dad for the flowers he'd sent her for her birthday. There was a message from Mrs. D'Ary—some athletic wear company was interested in having Neil do a spot for them and he needed to get home right away. And there was a message from Cara Benoit.

"Hello Jacy, Dakota. It's Cara. It's Thursday . . ."

"Yesterday," Dakota said.

"Hush," I snapped at him.

"Sorry."

"We're in Billings. Your dad's doing better today. He wants me to tell you to bring his schedule book and his checkbook if you come . . ."

"*If* we come," I muttered indignantly. "Like we wouldn't—"

"Hush," Dakota snapped at me.

I had to smile.

". . . he'll need to cancel the next couple of hikes. He's got pneumonia and was pretty bad when we first got here, but he's doing better today."

"She said that already," Dakota said.

I didn't tell him to hush. "She sounds exhausted."

He nodded.

Cara finished her message by telling us which room in which hospital Dad was in and saying again that he was doing better.

"Do you suppose Pastor Adams will let us ride down with him?" I asked Dakota. I had a learner's permit but not a license. "Or should I call Gary to see if he's got a wrecker run down there?"

"We'll ask Pastor Adams first." Dakota rubbed his finger along the top of the telephone receiver. "Cara would've called again if Dad had gotten worse again or—"

"I'm sure," I said quickly. "Let's go help Pastor Adams. I think we should get everything cleaned up before we leave so Dad won't have anything to do when he comes home."

"Okay." Dakota stood there with his finger still on the telephone receiver.

I stepped forward, gave him a nervous hug, and then left the office.

Group by group, the hikers finished unloading their packs and walked out to their vehicles with their original luggage in hand. The newlyweds first. Then the two men from Germany. The Sullivans. I thanked each of them for hiking with us, invited them to come for another trip anytime, and gave them complimentary *Back Trails Unlimited* T-shirts (instead of letting them know that they were available to buy) because they'd been so supportive of Dakota and me during Dad's absence.

I nearly forgot to relay Neil's mother's message to him when he climbed up into his SUV, but seeing his athletic bag on the front passenger seat reminded me.

"Can I write to you?" he asked me after grimacing about the message.

"Sure." I smiled.

He turned his attention to his steering wheel. "Jacy," he said, "I know my dad and I made things harder on you guys this trip than they had to be, especially your dad, and—"

"Don't worry about it, okay?" I tapped his door and stepped back. "I'm glad you two have started talking."

He nodded. "Me too."

"Don't forget my T-shirt," I shouted at the back of his 4 × 4 and then smiled and waved at Mr. D'Ary as he passed by me in his big fancy shiny black car.

For the next three hours, Dakota, Pastor Adams, Ezra, and I worked. Dakota shook out and put away all the empty packs. I washed, dried, and put away all the pots, pans, silverware, plates, cups, and canteens. Pastor Adams and Ezra set up all the tents in the grass in front of the house, swept them out, took them down again, and hung them to air out (along with their bags of poles and stakes) from the S-hooks Dad had screwed into one of the log ceiling beams in the supply room. I cleaned the foil cookstove burner wraps and repacked the stoves in their boxes while Dakota and Ezra hung the sleeping bags (which I would wash when we returned home) and their sacks over the two metal closet poles Dad had hung along the back wall. Pastor Adams unhitched the trailer and took our van into Cooke City to refuel it.

I went to my room, packed a small bag with "city" clothes, and hurried into the bathroom for a quick shower which turned into a long one simply because it was my first in six days and there was absolutely nothing like a shower after backpacking. All the smells washing off—insect repellent, dirt, sunscreen, sweat, and the most pungent of all of them, campfire smoke. And then the smells of soap and shampoo, and the refreshing feel of them on my skin and in my hair.

With some clean clothes, a quick visit with a brush, and a little bit of lotion for my hands, I felt presentable again. Human.

"Ezra's going to drive our pickup and I'll drive your dad's van," Pastor Adams told me when I'd gone downstairs again. "That way your dad'll be able to get you guys back home when he's well enough."

"Okay."

"It's already seven-thirty," he said. "It's three hours to Billings? Maybe a little longer once it's dark?"

"Yeah," I said. "Lots of deer to watch out for."

"We're all tired," he said. "What if we hang out here tonight, eat a good dinner, get a good night's sleep, and head out at first light? I know you want to get to your dad as soon as possible, but—"

I'd called Cara at the hospital and she'd told me that Dad was still sleeping most of the time but was out of imminent danger, so I forced myself to accept Pastor Adams's suggestion without argument. "No. I mean, yeah, I do. But what you said is smart." *I guess.* I grabbed my sweater from its hook near the front door. It was getting chilly already now that the sun had gone behind the mountain. "I'll go fix us something to eat."

Pastor Adams placed his hand on my shoulder and shook his head. "We'll go into Cooke City. You're as tired as the rest of us. Just let me grab a shower? I might frighten someone otherwise."

I laughed. "Okay."

He turned and started walking up the stairs.

"Pastor Adams?"

He stopped on the landing and looked at me.

"I . . . you've . . ." I shook my head and started again. "I don't know how to thank you for all you've done."

"It's not necessary," he said. "Friends help one another."

Friends.

The nature of our business and Dad's somewhat antagonistic attitude tended to foster civil but impersonal associations with people. We had accumulated acquaintances and customers over the years . . . plenty of them . . . but not *friends.*

Somehow, though, Pastor Adams had bypassed all that.

Was it really as elementary as the fact that he too had lost his wife?

I didn't think so.

What was it he had said that afternoon when I'd scolded him about getting after my father with all his God-stuff?

I know that God is trying to get your dad's attention. He tries to draw all of us to Himself.

Yes. That was what he'd said. As much as I was disinclined to admit it and afraid to embrace it, I no longer doubted that that was exactly what had been happening.

With Dad. And with me.

The television in Dad's room was on with the volume muted. Cara Benoit sat in a chair at the right of Dad's bed, sleeping. Her left ankle, which had been put in a knee-high walking cast, was propped up on a pillow on a second chair. The top of the small table beside Cara was cluttered with a crossword puzzle book, a pencil, her Bible, and a clear pitcher half-full of ice chips.

"Ezra and I are going to take our stuff home and come back," Pastor Adams whispered to Dakota and me and then the two of them quietly left the room.

We'd already spoken with the nurse and with Dad's doctor. They had taken him off oxygen that morning and were hopeful that he wouldn't need to be put back on it. He'd need to stay in the hospital at least another couple of days, but they expected him to continue to steadily improve.

"If this is what improved looks like," Dakota whispered to me, "I'm glad I wasn't here to see what he looked like when they thought he was bad."

I told him to be quiet, but did not dispute his observation.

Dad looked awful. Still. Ashen. Working hard just to breathe.

I'd always read in novels where people looked small when they were ill, and I thought I could remember thinking that of my mother the one time Dad had taken me to see her before she died—it had all happened so suddenly. But at six foot four and with a build consistent with his lifestyle of hiking miles and miles in the high country with an eighty-pound pack on his back, it would take a lot more than a case of pneumonia to stamp the word "small" on my father. He was as big and strong looking as ever except for his color and his stillness, and except for the fact that he was lying in a hospital bed with what his doctor called "fiber-like fluid" plugging his lungs and making him sound as if he was trying to breathe through shaving cream.

I walked around the empty side of his bed, sat carefully beside him, and took his hand in mine. It was cool.

No more fever, at least.

Dad opened his eyes right away at my touch, and I felt better as soon as he did. He looked alive with his eyes open and somehow not nearly as pale.

"Hey," he whispered to me.

"Hey." I leaned forward and kissed his forehead.

"You made it," he said.

I smiled. "Didn't I tell you we would?"

"You did."

"You're not supposed to talk much," Dakota reminded him as he walked around the bed and sat beside me.

"So talk to me," he said. "How'd it go?"

Cara woke up shortly after that while Dakota was in the middle of telling Dad about the "monster" brook trout—the largest he'd ever seen, anyway—that one of the guys from Germany had pulled out of Rainbow Lake. She insisted that Dakota and I both come over and hug her, which we did.

"Did you bring my books?" Dad asked me.

"Yeah," I told him. "But they can wait."

"The next hike's in a week," he said. "I've got to let—"

"Dad, I'll take care of it."

"He's horrible," Cara said. She smiled, but I didn't doubt that Dad had given her plenty of reason, even in his weakened condition, to be frustrated. Nobody would ever stamp the words "co-operative patient" on Hayden Craig either.

Dad was released from the hospital early Tuesday morning, but we decided to take Pastor Adams up on an offer to "hang out" with him and Ezra in Billings for a few days. We could do our winter shopping. We could visit Custer Battlefield. We could eat at a restaurant that didn't have log walls. We could sit in traffic or wait in line to buy toilet paper and a couple packages of pencils and be reminded of just how thankful we were that we lived somewhere remote.

We could keep Dad from doing anything strenuous.

We could . . . "Go to church?" I stared across the dinner table Thursday evening in disbelief at my father. "You want to go to church?"

Cara Benoit laughed. She had phoned her brother when she and Dad had arrived in Billings and he'd come for Emily, but their scheduled flight wasn't due to leave until Monday morning. She had decided to wait for it. Pastor Adams had arranged accommodations for her at the home of one of the families who attended his church—though she was spending most of her time with us. "It's not that bad, Jacy," she said.

"Yeah," Ezra agreed. "Dad's a great preacher. You should hear him."

I smiled. I'd heard him. That wasn't the issue in question. I looked at Dad again. *You want to go to church?*

"A person should try it at least once," he said quietly.

"Well," I said, "okay, if that's what you want. But I don't have a dress." I laughed. "I mean, I don't even own one."

"You don't own a dress?" Cara blurted and then quickly looked apologetically at my father.

He stabbed at his corn with his fork. "Where would she wear one?"

"To . . . church . . . Sunday morning." Cara stared down at her corn.

"Okay," Dad said. "So I'll get her a dress. She . . . should have a dress."

Cara nodded but still didn't look up at him. "Good."

Wondering what on earth had just happened between my father and Cara Benoit and having no particular desire to own a dress, I said, "You guys, it's no big deal. I'm sure they won't kick me out if I'm not in a dress." I turned to look at Pastor Adams. "Right?"

"Right," he said. He was smiling as he looked down at *his* corn.

I started laughing—these adults were behaving so strangely—but stopped because Dad started coughing. I supposed I should have gotten used to it after the past few days, but it still frightened me. I was glad that we weren't at home where Dakota and I would have to take care of him alone.

Cara reached into Dad's shirt pocket and pulled out the inhaler the doctor had prescribed for him. "Breathe it in slowly," she told him. Her hand remained firmly on his shoulder while he did.

When he'd finished, he stood and said, "I'm going to go outside for a minute." Then he looked at me. "Come with me, Jace?"

"Sure."

Pastor Adams had neither a front porch nor a deck, but he did have six cement steps and a small landing so we sat there.

"You okay?" I asked Dad.

He ignored the question. He was as okay as anyone would be two days out from being hospitalized with pneumonia. "Jacy," he said, "I wonder, uh, how many other things I've overlooked taking care of for you on account of I'm not a woman and I didn't think of it."

"This is about the dress?"

He nodded.

"Dad, I don't need a dress. Like you said, where would I wear one?"

"Your mother would have made sure you had places to wear one," he said. "You'd be in school. You'd have a boyfriend maybe. You'd play the flute." He shrugged. "I don't know where you'd wear one, but she would have. And if I hadn't been so busy trying not to think about her then—"

"Dad . . ." I laughed. "Play the *flute?*"

He smiled.

Good. "I'm happy doing what we're doing." I stared at him until he turned and looked directly at me. "Okay?"

"Okay."

I turned my attention to the street again and leaned against Dad's shoulder. Billings was so noisy. Even here at Pastor Adams's house, which was in a residential neighborhood several blocks from any "busy" streets, my thinking was constantly being intruded upon by noise. Car noise. People noise. Dog noise. The noise of construction somewhere. A truck was backing up in one of the driveways down the block . . . *beep beep beep beep.* Sprinklers were on in the yard across the street. A group of pre-teen boys rode by on bicycles laughing profanities at one another. A stereo blared nearby.

But the evening air was cool and relatively fresh and I enjoyed a "quiet" few minutes with Dad before he decided we needed to go inside and help Pastor Adams clear the table.

It wasn't until several hours later when I was lying alone in the dark of one of Pastor Adams's downstairs guest rooms—being kept awake by the traffic noise outside the window—that my mind fastened on the rest of what Dad had been trying to say when I'd interrupted him to laugh about playing the flute.

And if I hadn't been so busy trying not to think about her then . . .

Obviously Dad had been busy recently trying *to* think about things. Equally as obvious was his response to all that thinking.

Insecurity.

But if my father could truly face his life instead of always trying to avoid and outmaneuver his feelings about it, maybe he'd finally be able to find peace as Pastor Adams had. Then hurt over Mom would never again have the power to sneak up on him and disarm him the way it could now.

And what about me?

I felt as if I'd always been fairly honest with myself about my life. I enjoyed it. I loved Dad and Dakota. I'd never want to live in a city like Billings. It didn't bother me that much that our situation wasn't typical. I did acknowledge and allow some emptiness over the fact that I no longer had a mom. I told myself often that I wasn't afraid to face anything, and yet . . .

I'd been terrified during Dad's absence on the trail. Lying awake like an idiot with my hand on his gun, wishing he was there to protect me. True, I had pulled it together, but it alarmed me that I'd allowed it to come apart in the first place.

And then there was the whole God-question.

I'd been running from it as if it were a starved grizzly after me, claws and teeth out, ready to rip me open and eat me whole.

Why? Because it might require some changes to my thinking?

Because I didn't want to deal with the issue of my mother's eternity since she hadn't known Him?

Because in order to embrace it I'd have to admit out loud that I too had need? I wasn't sure.

One thing was certain though. I could no longer appease myself with the idea, the excuse, that there couldn't be a loving God behind our horrible world. Pastor Adams's reasoning on the issue had seen to that. More than that, his life had. His world had been plenty horrible recently, and yet the effects, influence, and proofs of a loving God were all around him. There to be seen by someone daring enough to be honest about what she was seeing.

Someone like me?

At Cara Benoit's insistence Dad only got as far as the parking lot the next morning on his mission to take me to the mall to find a dress.

"You'll be completely out of place in a dress shop, Hayden," she told him. "And anyway, you're not supposed to overdo it. Let me go with her. Do you know how long it can take a woman to find just the right dress? Hours of traipsing through the mall—"

"Clumping along in your walking cast," Dad interjected.

He stumped Cara for only an instant. "We'll rent a wheel-chair."

"Dad, Cara's right." I leaned forward between the two front seats so that we wouldn't have to talk at one another in the rear-view mirror. "You've been coughing a lot this morning again. Go back to Pastor Adams's house, take a nap, and come back for us later."

Dad did not agree easily, but he did agree. And he said as I jumped out of the van behind Cara, "Your mother used to put you in burgundy velvet a lot."

So Cara and I spent the morning looking for a burgundy—though not necessarily velvet—dress.

When we'd found one, one we both liked and thought Dad would like too, along with a slip, nylons, a pair of black low-heeled shoes, and a fine gold necklace to wear with it, Cara said that she was starving and ordered me to wheel her into the near-est sit-down restaurant.

It happened to be a Greek place, which suited both of us.

While we waited for our food to be brought to our table, we talked and laughed about everything from the weather to what Cara thought her students would say when she told them how she'd broken her ankle.

"I really don't know what I would have done if your father hadn't come over to help us," she said after we'd gone silent for the first time.

"Well," I said, "I've got to tell you that knowing you were going to stay with him and make sure he got taken care of while we were gone pulled me through not knowing how he was doing."

She nodded. "He was so sick by the time we got off that mountain that Todd even stayed with us that first night and day in Billings until he was less critical."

"I don't think I want to know the details," I told her quietly. Honestly.

She nodded. "The important thing is that he's going to be fine."

"Right," I said. "And that he wasn't alone. That really means a lot to me, Cara, and I don't think I'll ever be able to thank you enough for that."

"Oh, you don't have to thank me." She grinned and then looked to be reconsidering. "Well, now that you mention it, he really was kind of a pain. He could get his own ice, thanks." She laughed and then deepened her voice to imitate Dad. "If you're going to sit there and read that thing in front of me, Cara, you could at least read so I can hear you, thanks. I have enough blankets, thanks. Would you stop telling me how to breathe? I've been doing it since I was born. Thanks." She tapped the tabletop. "He is the classic strong man who'd rather spend six hours trying to figure out how to install his own septic system pump in the dark of night in the middle of winter than call someone to do it in the morning."

"He calls it self-reliance," I told her.

131

"I know," she said. "We discussed that. We discussed a lot of things, and the really great part was that I could get the nurses on my side telling him that he wasn't allowed to talk back."

"So . . . what did you tell him? About self-reliance?"

"I read a Scripture to him," she said. "One that I need to remember quite frequently in my own life because I tend to be kind of a self-reliant person too." She leaned back from the table when the man came with our baskets. After thanking him and asking a blessing over the food—something I was still struggling to remember to pause for—she said, "I like to do things for myself. I like to know that I can do them for myself. I usually can do them for myself. And when I can't, I absolutely hate asking for help."

I took a bite of my fried bread and grimaced at the tartness of the dressing they'd smeared all over it. "That sounds like Dad," I said, and then I grabbed my glass for a sip of water. "God thinks that's a bad thing?"

"Not necessarily," she said. "He wants us to work and to do our best at whatever our hand finds to do. But the main step we have to take in coming to know Him and then moving on to walk with Him is acknowledging our need for Him. That can be hard to do for a person like your dad." She shrugged. "I know it was hard for me. I wanted to get right with God for myself first and then approach Him. The only problem is, we can't do that. We only get right with Him when we allow Him to come into our lives and cleanse and use us."

I thought about that for several minutes while we ate and concluded that it did make sense. Even if I determined that I wanted to do the right thing from here on out, I'd surely botch it. Probably before the end of the day. I wouldn't know how to figure out what God wanted me to do in every given instance, let alone how He wanted me to do it. Even if I could come up with the knowing, there'd be the problem of actually *doing* it each and every time. And even if I did manage to manage all that, something would still need to be done about all the things I'd done wrong in my past. They'd need to be erased, somehow. Removed from my current portfolio.

And God would do that . . . if I'd get off my high horse and ask Him to. That's what Pastor Adams had been telling us. That's what Cara was telling me now.

"What was the verse you read to my father?" I asked her.

"Psalm 20, verses 6, 7 and 8," she said. "It says, *Now know I that the Lord saveth His anointed; he will hear him from his holy heaven with the saving strength of his right hand. Some trust in chariots, and some in horses: but we will remember the name of the Lord our God. They are brought down and fallen: but we are risen, and stand upright.*"

I thought of Neil D'Ary. He had a great tennis game to trust in. Lots of money. A father who would never sit back and watch him throw his opportunities away. And yet "brought down" and "fallen" were two words that could definitely be used to describe him.

I thought of my father. Physically strong. In control of a successful business. He could count on my love and on Dakota's. He was mentally determined to not cave under his pain. And yet . . . "brought down" and "fallen" could just as easily apply to him as to Neil.

I thought of Pastor Adams. He'd suffered the same loss as my father. His job couldn't be all that easy with the number of churches out there for people to choose from. And yet he had definitely "risen" above all that and could still "stand upright."

Then I thought of myself.

"Cara," I said, "there's part of me that wants to believe that God is real and cares about me and can make my life into something that counts for more than just me. But . . ." I raised my hands and lowered them to the table again in frustration. "I just . . ."

Did I really want to own up to my deepest point of need in front of this woman?

Cara gave me the time I needed to decide.

Finally I said, "I really don't remember my mom. I think maybe I let myself forget on purpose, you know? And with Dad always being so silent about her, it was easy to do. Maybe I even convinced myself that it was the right thing to do. I don't remember now. I was only seven. Who knows how a seven-year-old really thinks? But I do remember that I loved her. And I remember that she . . . she never talked about God. He's never been part of who we are. So . . . where is she, Cara?"

"Where is she? Jacy, that's a question only God can answer."

"She'd have to be in hell."

There. I'd said it. I recalled attributing this concern to my father during his conversation with Pastor Adams that first day of our hike, which seemed in a way like it had happened in another lifetime now. But he'd never said it was a concern of his. Not to me, or to Pastor Adams, or to anyone else. For all I really knew, it may never even have occurred to him.

"I remember being so scared," I told Cara in practically a whisper, "because Dad couldn't tell me where she was. But now, not knowing is way less scary than thinking about her being in hell."

Cara pushed her basket aside to take my hands in both of hers. She looked directly at me. "Honey, I want you to remember three things. One is that God is a just God. He knew whether your mother had looked to Him or not. The fact that you don't know if she did doesn't necessarily mean that she didn't." She paused for a couple of seconds. "Two, even if your mother did reject Him and is in hell, which I'm not saying she is because God's the only one Who knows that, but if she is . . . it can't be changed now. Somehow, in heaven with God, your tears over her eternity along with your tears over everything else are going to be wiped away. I don't know how He's going to accomplish that, but that's what His Word says. You won't live forever with that fear or that grief."

I looked down at our hands when tears pushed their way to my eyes.

Cara found my napkin underneath my basket and handed it to me. "The third thing I want you to remember is this. If God is calling you now, drawing you to Him, you are accountable for what you know *now*. Not for what you knew before He reached out to you. You can't go back to when you'd never sensed His realness. You won't be able to tell Him that you honestly never knew, because He brings us to a position where He reveals Himself to us beyond the step of believing He might exist to the turning point of knowing He's real."

I nodded. That pivotal "point of faith" that Pastor Adams had mentioned to my father.

For the first time during our conversation, it occurred to me that I was crying like a loser in a public restaurant in the middle of a public mall with a great many members of that public watching on.

Strangely, though, I didn't care.

After dinner that night at Pastor Adams's house, I volunteered Dad to run Cara back to the home where she was staying and then informed him that I'd be riding along with them. I wanted to thank Cara for not telling anyone about our conversation at the Greek restaurant until after I'd had a chance to talk with Dad . . . which was what I intended to do once he and I were alone.

"Can we drive for a while, Dad?" I asked him when I climbed into the front passenger seat of our van after coming back from helping Cara to her door. "Away from the city lights? I want to look at the stars."

"All right."

"I found a dress today," I told him.

"Good," he said.

"It's burgundy."

"Good," he said again, but not as quickly.

"Are you feeling okay, Dad?"

He laughed. "What's this about, Jace?"

There was no sense in trying to deceive him. "I want to talk to you about something, but not till we stop. Okay?"

"All right." His hands tightened a bit on the steering wheel as he made himself more comfortable in his seat. "Yes. I'm feeling okay."

"You really scared me," I admitted.

He glanced at me and then turned his attention back to the road. "I scared myself, to be honest."

"Cara said you were really bad when you first got in to Billings."

"I don't doubt it," he said. "I don't remember getting to Billings. I remember looking over at Kersey Lake with Todd saying something to me and then waking up trying to get these tubes away from my face and Cara leaning over me with her hand over mine telling me that they were there to help me breathe and that I had to trust her and leave them alone." He shrugged. "Then I kind of figured out what must be going on, but it was a little unsettling at first not remembering how I'd gotten there or knowing for sure where I was."

"I'm glad Cara was with you," I said. "I mean since Dakota and I couldn't be."

"How'd you feel about doing the trail without me?" he wanted to know.

I pulled in a long breath. "I think that if I'd been doing it for any other reason than because you were sick, and if I wasn't worried about you, it would have been kind of exciting in its own way. Like a test or something."

"I'm real proud of you and Dakota," he said.

His quiet praise meant everything to me. But I didn't know how to say so without sounding stupid, so I kept staring straight ahead and said nothing.

"I might have to start letting you two run some of the one-or two-day hikes," he said after a while. "Work myself into letting you do the long ones eventually."

"While you sit home and read the funnies?" I laughed. "Like that's ever going to happen!"

"No, see, we could run two trips at a time then, a couple days apart." He grinned. "Either that or I'll just go fishing."

I punched his arm. "You'd go crazy after about two days of that."

"I know it. I'm just about going crazy now and I have a reason not to be working."

"You'll be hunting this fall," I reminded him, and then told him that he had lots of new messages at home.

We drove up Airport Road, which had been cut into the side of the rimrocks on the north end of Billings, past the airport, and northwest out of town. The city lights below us to our left in the ancient Yellowstone River Valley were stunning, but not nearly so much as the huge sky full of stars that we could see once Dad clicked off the headlights a mile or so into a gravel county road that he'd found.

"It's almost more amazing than at home," I said, "because there are no trees to look between."

"Nothing but sky," Dad agreed. "Want to walk a bit?"

I smiled. What could be more perfect? We wouldn't even have to worry about bears. "Sure."

Gravel crunched beneath our feet as we walked along the road that we could just barely distinguish in the light of the stars and from a low crescent moon. The sounds of night were different here than in the mountains. A gentle breeze, instead of wind, blew along the tips of the tall dry prairie grasses instead of through the tops of the trees. There was no echo, only huge empty space. And there was a constant hum of insects.

"What did you want to talk to me about, Jace?" Dad asked me. He sounded a little nervous.

I stepped closer to him. I'd thought of several different ways that I could word my news during the evening, but none of them seemed appropriate here in the actual moment. I licked my lips and just said it. Flat-out. No preamble. No explanation afterwards.

"I asked Cara to pray with me to accept Christ today."

Dad said nothing. Ten steps. Twenty.

"Are you mad?" I asked him.

"No," he said. Then he laughed. "I guess if you had to choose between getting me mad at you or God, you made the smarter decision." Then he took my hand in his. "But I know it wasn't about that."

"No. It wasn't about that at all."

"I guess all Bruce's talking got to you?"

"It made sense," I admitted. "But I think it was actually God that got to me in the end."

"That's how Cara told me it would be," Dad said.

We walked for almost half an hour along that dark gravel road. Talking. Not talking. Talking again. I told my father quietly that I'd buried my fears about Mom having been taken away from me so deeply inside myself that it had taken his illness—and the resulting fear that he might be taken away from me too, to get me to be honest about them.

"I'd looked to you to be that constant in my universe that could never be taken away from me," I told him. "But you can't be."

"No," he said. "I can't. Just like your mother couldn't be that for me even though I needed her to."

"But God is," I said. "Pastor Adams told me that one night at the campfire. That I could always count on Him. I wasn't sure I believed him then, but now I know it's true."

"That would have to be a God-thing," Dad said. "Being able to 'know' like that."

As we walked back toward our van, I sensed, in Dad's silences and where he chose to take them more so than in anything he said, that he was battling and maybe resisting a God-thing of his own. I could only hope that when he came to the point of making his decision about it one way or the other that he would decide as I had.

But I didn't feel the need to try to persuade him to even though I wished I could. Dad already knew all the details of salvation. He'd read the whole Bible and had been discussing it with

Pastor Adams and Cara Benoit. The only thing he lacked was believing it. For real. For him.

That part was God's job, and because of the way He had so gently and competently convinced me, I didn't fear entrusting my father to Him.

Our mutual Father.

We rode back to Billings mainly in silence. But as we looked down on the city lights again, Dad laughed a little and said, "I don't suppose I'll be backing out of going to church Sunday morning now."

I grinned. "Not a chance."

When I walked into the dining room Sunday morning, I was so consumed with anticipation to go to church that I would have missed everyone's reaction to seeing me in a dress for the first time if Ezra hadn't stopped talking to his father to tell me how great I looked.

"Thank you," I said. I spun around once—because it seemed like the thing to do—and then glanced across the room at my father.

He'd been doing some shopping too, I noticed. Probably because he'd only had the clothes on his back and in his backpack when he'd arrived in Billings. Camping clothes. Jeans. T-shirts. Flannel shirts. Hiking boots. Now he was wearing tan dress pants, a crisp teal dress shirt, and a tie!

I smiled. "I've never seen you in a tie."

"You have," he said. "You just don't remember. I used to wear suits and ties all the time when I worked at the office."

"I guess I don't remember," I confessed. "You look real good." And he did. Not only because of his clothes, but because his color had been improving consistently over the past few days so that this morning he looked almost healthy again.

"So do you," he said.

"She looks like a girl," Dakota muttered. "What's the big deal?" He stomped over to the table, sat down, helped himself to some eggs without having been welcomed to them, and then began eating before any of the rest of us had seated ourselves and before Pastor Adams had asked the blessing.

Dad started to say something to Dakota. I caught a flash of what it might be in the tightness of his jaw, but Pastor Adams held up his hand and shook his head.

It's okay, Hayden. He doesn't understand. It scares him.

My brother had not been responding well to the changes going on inside Dad and me even though I'd done my best a couple of times to explain them to him. As far as he was concerned, all this God-stuff was nothing more than a primitive salve for the hurts of desperate people. An emotional bandage, sling, crutch. He wanted no part of going to church, though he would be going because Dad had decided that we'd go as a family. He'd pretty much quit talking to Pastor Adams altogether and had nothing but criticism to hurl at Ezra. He still behaved civilly toward Cara Benoit because she'd been such a help to Dad when he was sick, but even that was wearing thin.

I walked over to the table and sat in the chair nearest him. I understood his feelings. I'd shared them as recently as a week and a half ago. But he was just going to have to adjust because his pouting and antagonism would never be able to reverse the things that God had set in motion in my heart and life.

I knew that things would be challenging for me once Dad and Dakota and I were home again that evening. I would miss Cara, Ezra, and Pastor Adams. More than that, there'd be the return of the routine of my life before being God's. There'd be nobody to compel me to think about Him if I chose not to.

But Ezra had given me a Bible, and had pointed out the section in the back that included several different strategies and suggestions for reading it through. Pastor Adams had given me a new believer's journal and study guide to complete with the suggestion that Dad might be willing to do some of the lessons with me. Cara had given me the promise that she would call and write frequently.

It all helped.

So did God Himself.

During the final three weeks of the summer tourist season, Dakota and I stayed busy running day hikes while Dad remained at the house resting, seeing to the mechanical and maintenance needs of our snowmobiles and putting details together for our fall and winter trips. It seemed that on every trip I led, at least one of the customers would mention God or church or creation science or *something* that would clue me in to the fact that he shared my faith. Dakota would usually grimace in frustration whenever this happened, but now I considered it a direct provision of God. I was meeting other Christians from all over the country. It amazed me that even though some of them had different ideas about some things than Pastor Adams or Cara had had, basically, when it came right down to what we'd put our trust in, we could always enjoy excellent and encouraging conversation.

Dad did do some of the lessons in my new believer's study with me. What gratified me even more than that though, was his effort to be more honest with himself about what was inside him. He'd pulled three boxes from the attic . . . boxes I never knew existed . . . boxes of Mom's things. Quilts she'd made. Some of her clothes. Photo albums. Her violin. He'd shown them to Dakota and me, and he'd even allowed me to keep one of the quilts for my bed. If Dakota or I asked him how he was doing when he was obviously feeling sad or angry or alone, he'd begun to attempt to tell us. Sometimes he couldn't. Sometimes he'd just say, "I don't want to talk about it." But he had quit saying, "I'm okay" or "Just tired" or "Headache."

I was incredibly proud of him.

Acknowledging weakness took a lot of strength for someone like my father.

One evening at the beginning of September we drove in to Cooke City for dinner. Dad would be leaving to guide four men from North Carolina on a four-day bow hunt in a couple of days, and he wanted to go over the schedule he expected us to maintain at home. Firewood needed to be chopped and stacked. Joe Sutter would be bringing his horses up at the end of the week for the next trip on the books—an elk hunt that all three of us would be doing with a group of six of Dad's CPA "pals" from Milwaukee. He had preprepared all of our school lessons and wanted to be sure we knew how much he had in mind for us to complete.

"Plus," he told us while we were waiting for our steaks, "I have a surprise for you two."

"A surprise?" I grinned. I couldn't remember the last time Dad had had a "surprise" for us.

"Yep." He reached into his jacket pocket and pulled out a stack of brochures from instantly recognizable places. "You guys knew that Cara Benoit lives in Florida?"

I shook my head. In all the conversations Cara and I had had, her place of residence had never come up.

"She mentioned to me while I was in the hospital under strict instructions not to talk back that while I might think of our life as a perpetual vacation, you two might like to see something different."

That sounded like something Cara would say when Dad wouldn't be able to argue.

Dad smiled at my smile. "Yeah. Anyway, her brother called me a couple weeks ago and told me that he'd like us to come and stay with them this winter sometime and go see some of the things there are to see in Florida."

"Emily's dad? He doesn't have to do that. It's not like we did anything that anyone else wouldn't have done." Dakota picked up one of the brochures. One with a picture of a huge roller-coaster on its cover. "Wow!"

"So what do you think?" Dad asked me. What Dakota thought was already more than adequately observable.

"I think it would be great," I said. "Will Cara be there too?"

Dad laughed. "Do you really think she'd allow me to bring you to Florida and not plan on her seeing you?" He took a sip of his coffee. "She'll be teaching during the week, but she's going to meet up with us at her brother's house for the weekend. We've got ten days."

I thought of Neil D'Ary. Now he wouldn't be the only one soaking up the sun in the middle of winter. I'd have to add this piece of information in a PS at the bottom of my reply to the letter he'd sent me. He had inquired about Dad's health, and about how early and how deep it snowed up at our place, and about our hike schedule for the next summer. I'd answered his questions, had asked a few of my own, and had then written the largest chunk of the letter recounting my decision to become a Christian. I knew that Neil had spoken with Pastor Adams during the hike about his relationship with his father, but I wasn't sure whether Pastor Adams had told Neil how he could have peace with God through salvation . . . so I did. Just in case. After all, there was no guarantee of another opportunity. Neil might forget all about me once he returned to tennis and all the pretty and sophisticated city girls screaming his name wherever he went.

I leaned back in my chair. "Ten days in warm sunny Florida," I said to Dad. "I think I might be able to suffer through that."

While Dad and Dakota perused the brochures and tried to agree upon the places we simply had to see, I looked over both of their heads at the four roughly framed photographs the restaurant owner had recently hung on one of the thick varnished log ceiling beams. The first was an aerial view of one of the switchback sections of the Beartooth Highway. The next one was of a griz pawing at a dumpster. The third one was of a school bus buried to its window tops in snow in front of the Cooke City General Store. The fourth and final one was of someone placing a rock on that "monument" at the Continental Divide.

How many people throughout the world had a similar photograph, I wondered. I knew two guys from Germany who each had one, and those were just the most recent of the tens of photographs that I personally had taken at the spot.

Hundreds, potentially thousands, of people had had their picture taken there. *Been there. Done that. Look, Aunt Marge . . . I*

145

stepped over the Divide. All in honor of an imaginary line on a map. An imaginary line that marked the place where my God had decided to send the waters going east or west.

I took a sip of my water and considered the other divide I had stepped over recently. The divide between unbelief and belief. The divide between not knowing God and knowing Him. The divide between eternal separation from God and eternal life in Him. There was no monument to put a rock on. There was no photograph to hang on the wall. There was nothing to brag about to Aunt Marge or anyone else . . . though there was definitely something to tell.

It was an event, a moment of decision, that had changed my life—changed me—forever. And the best part was that I was only at the beginning of everything that awaited me on the other side of that divide, and I couldn't wait to see and experience the rest of it.

One step at a time, like hiking the trail.